DOCTOR WHO
SILVER NEMESIS

GW00399914

DOCTOR WHO
SILVER NEMESIS

based on the BBC television series by Kevin Clarke
by arrangement with BBC Books, a division of BBC
Enterprises Ltd

KEVIN CLARKE

Number 143 in the
Target Doctor Who Library

TARGET

This edition first published in Great Britain in 1993 by
Target Books
An imprint of Virgin Publishing Ltd
332 Ladbroke Grove
London W10 5AH

First published in Great Britain 1989

Novelization copyright © Kevin Clarke 1989
Original script copyright © Kevin Clarke 1988
'Doctor Who' series copyright © British Broadcasting
Corporation 1988, 1989

The BBC producer was John Nathan-Turner
The director was Chris Clough
The role of the Doctor was played by Sylvester McCoy

Printed and bound in Great Britain by
Cox & Wyman Ltd, Reading, Berks.

ISBN 0 426 20340 2

This book is sold subject to the condition that
it shall not, by way of trade or otherwise,
be lent, re-sold, hired out, or otherwise circulated
without the publisher's prior consent in
any form of binding or cover other than that in
which it is published and without a similar
condition including this condition being imposed upon the
subsequent purchaser

For
D H F Somerset
with all my gratitude

1

The closer one travels towards it from the cold silent darkness of infinite space, the more the planet Earth appears as a backcloth to some small theatrical performance taking place on a limited budget. From the tiny distance of only a few million miles, approached directly, the little production looms confusedly, the seas and land masses cheap dye, dampened and imperceptibly merging one into the other.

Towards this tiny but slowly growing scene, what appears at first to be a ball of rock shoots through the darkness. It might be taken for a comet, one of the endless number of pebbles or worlds passing eternally through space, until viewed from a few hundred miles. When seen from perhaps the distance which separates London and Berlin, a small tail of flame becomes visible, spraying from behind the rock. It might simply be a natural discharge of gases self-igniting, yet there is a quality of precision about the flame which invites further examination. It proves from a closer viewpoint to be not one, but four small jets of fire.

The Earth looms steadily larger with a slow inevitability as the rock flies towards it, apparently propelled by four small rockets fixed to a kind of sled at its base. The comet might thus appear to be the creation of some enthusiastic amateur with an interest in space travel. It is certainly a ramshackle enough device.

As it passes on, inexorably towards the looming Earth, something else about it momentarily catches the attention. Despite the speed at which the comet – if that is what it is – passes, one might be forgiven for imagining one briefly glimpsed a face within the centre of the rock. Somehow, in that instant, there is the fleeting sense of a still expression, carved in silver. Perhaps it is seen through a small glass panel, or more likely, not seen at all.

Infinity of a more immediate nature was on the Doctor and Ace's minds that afternoon. In the case of the Doctor, a number of simultaneous infinities were at work, all of them pleasurable on this occasion. The rare appearance of the sun in England on a late summer's day seemed to be everlasting. The beautiful waterside garden of the pub outside which they were sitting equally seemed to be going nowhere, as indeed it had not for at least three hundred years. Of greatest importance to both of them was the jazz blowing out of the saxophone of, in the Doctor's view, the most exciting musical discovery since John Coltrane; it sounded and felt as infinite as anything the Doctor had ever encountered on his travels. He had once defined music to Ace as interior space travel, and he reflected on the accuracy of this remark as the drummer counted in the band for the final number of their first set.

8

The people around them were equally relaxed. The music blew through their souls and drifted gently away over the countryside. It would have required a cynic to pay more than passing attention to the two large men tapping their feet rather mechanically at the edge of the audience. Among civilized music lovers it would be almost unthinkable that anyone might stare at them, either because they were identical twins, or because while apparently listening to the band they both continued wearing what looked like extremely expensive personal stereo headphones – headphones that appeared to be made of solid silver. The crowd, however, were music lovers, and although the identical men were extremely large, no one did stare at them and such questions did not arise.

The final number came to an end. The crowd applauded, yelling for more, but the band took a break. Ace picked up an abandoned Sunday paper and stretched. 'I could listen to them all afternoon,' she said.

The Doctor opened his eyes dreamily, still out in the distant galactic reaches of the last high E flat.

'And so we shall,' he replied.

Fully aware of this, because more than cursory preparations had brought them here in the first place to catch the quartet, Ace was already immersed in the news. 'Have you seen this?' She rustled the paper at the Doctor. A headline 'Meteor approaches England' swam briefly before his eyes. 'Charlton have picked up three points.'

The Doctor nodded, seeming to concentrate fully on her excitement.

9

'Yes,' he agreed, 'that's my favourite kind of jazz: straight blowing. I'm afraid I got quite annoyed when it went through the audiophonic lasers phase.'

'Who are they?'

'You know.' It appeared she did not. 'Sound and light becoming the same thing.' He might as well have been speaking the lost and later corrupted, recycled and codified sound-patterns of the defunct planet Ofrix, to which no outside being other than himself, to his knowledge, had ever ventured. 'Holographic movies coming out of saxophones.' They appeared to have reached a communicatory impasse. The Doctor looked desperately at the date on the paper and beamed with relief. 'Oh, of course. It's 1988. Ten years to go. Make the most of them.'

Ace, as usual, was not fooled. The Doctor could see this. 'I complained about the future of jazz to Louis Armstrong,' he continued in a brave attempt to reassert his authority. It didn't do to let Ace see him slip up.

'What did he say?'

'I can't really remember. Oh, yes.' Recalling it, the Doctor warmed to his theme. 'He said music would always survive. He was right, of course. You see, he knew better than anyone that if you're going to play around with the most basic principles of time then mark my words time will – ' the Doctor was sharply interrupted by an unearthly screeching which seemed to come from inside his shirt-sleeve ' – catch up.'

People nearby turned round. The Doctor busied himself inside his jacket and the noise stopped.

'What's that?' asked Ace.

'Very strange. A reminder, of course.'

'Go on then.'

The Doctor was only too happy to do so. 'Well you see, Louis Armstrong . . .'

'I don't mean that. What about your alarm?'

'Oh that.' The Doctor shifted uncomfortably. There was a pause. 'What about it?' he attempted lightly.

Ace gave him one of her more direct looks. 'What's it supposed to remind you of?' she demanded relentlessly.

The Doctor prevaricated. 'Well obviously, I set it so that at this precise moment I would change course to . . . our new destination.'

Ace, however, was not satisfied. 'Where's that?' she insisted.

There was nothing else for it but the truth; often, in the Doctor's view, a mistake. 'I've forgotten,' he admitted.

Ace looked at him, knowing all too well what was coming. 'Oh, Professor . . .'

'Yes, you're quite right. I'm afraid we'll have to go and find out.'

He was already marching away among the tables towards the riverside path. Ace stopped to buy a souvenir cassette from the band and ran to catch up. In their hurry, neither of them noticed the two large men stand and follow.

The TARDIS waited among some trees across a small footbridge. Ace, reaching the Doctor, was still annoyed. She followed him on to the bridge.

It was at that moment that two simultaneous bursts of gunfire tore out of the bushes behind them. The

11

force of the bullets threw the Doctor and Ace headlong into the water.

The two large men emerged from the bushes, their silver headphones still in position. They watched silently as the unmoving bodies floated downstream.

In 1638 Lady Peinforte controlled her impatience with an effort, as she had been doing for many days. She aimed the arrow very carefully at the blackbird sitting in the tree and pulled back the bowstring. The bird sang on as she tautened the bow further; then she fired.

The arrow embedded itself in the trunk and the tree immediately emptied of birds. There was a nervous attempt at applause from behind her. Richard, her servant, smiled fulsomely. 'Oh very good, my lady.'

Ignoring him in disgust, she dropped the bow on to the ground and strode into the house. She had waited long enough.

Inside, an elderly man sat bent over scrolls of calculation muttering to himself.

'How much longer?' she demanded.

The elderly man continued muttering, absorbed in his work. Lady Peinforte seethed. The last servant who ignored her had suffered a number of torments that surprised even those familiar with her strict standards of etiquette. Richard, who had followed her in, was anxious to assist.

'He doesn't hear you ma'am,' he informed her needlessly. 'Shall I . . . ?'

'Leave him. There'll be time enough to punish his impertinence when he has finished.'

A pot of green liquid containing the floating remains of a blackened human hand simmered gently on the fire. Above it, a number of gold-tipped arrows were apparently drying. Lady Peinforte examined them carefully and held them out to Richard. 'Put these with the others,' she instructed.

Richard was nervous. Lady Peinforte glared at him. 'Are you so very feeble? The poison cannot harm unless the arrow's tip should break the skin. Let who will steal my gold.'

Richard turned to a silver arrow, lying in state on a purple cushion. 'And this one, my lady?'

'Leave that to me. You're sure the potion is well mixed?'

'On my life, ma'am.' Suddenly conscious that this was perhaps an unfortunate choice of phrase, Richard amended it to: 'I guarantee it.'

'Then we await but the calculation.' This was said emphatically, for the benefit of the elderly man, but he continued working, oblivious to her words.

Aware of this, Richard spoke quietly. 'There is but the final ingredient of the liquid wanting, as my lady knows. For that, I was thinking . . .'

He was interrupted by a cry from the elderly man at the table. 'My lady! Lady Peinforte: I've finished.'

Lady Peinforte gazed at him in disbelief. 'You have the answer?'

'Yes, my lady.'

'Quickly then. Tell me.'

The man fumbled among his scrolls and held up the final one. 'The comet Nemesis will circle the heavens every twenty-five years . . .'

13

Lady Peinforte cut in. 'I know this. When will it land?'

Heedless of the interruption, the elderly man rambled on: '. . . passing ever closer until it once again strikes Earth at the point of its original departure in the, ah, meadow outside.'

Lady Peinforte was beside herself. 'Yes, yes, *when?*'

There was a pause. The man found his place on the scroll. 'The, ah, twenty-third of November . . . nineteen hundred and eighty-eight.'

Lady Peinforte almost fainted. Her voice was weak. 'You are certain?'

'See for yourself, ma'am.' He handed her the last page of calculation. It swam before her eyes. Dimly, she was aware of his voice in the distance.

'My equations will have astounding applications! I can do anything!' the old man burbled. 'I shall build a flying machine. Imagine that, my lady. Human beings flying like birds. Let me see . . .' He returned to his figures and his voice faded away.

'Bring the cups of potion,' commanded Lady Peinforte. 'We leave at once.'

'The final ingredient, my lady,' Richard reminded her. 'Human blood.'

'I shall change the world . . .' murmured the elderly mathematician.

'Ah yes, Richard,' replied Lady Peinforte, softly. 'Close the door.'

The enormous drawing room of the former German colonial residence was filled, as it normally was, with sunlight and the chatter of birds from the forest that

14

surrounded it for many miles in every direction. The South American heat was as intense as usual, but after these many years, the man known as Herr De Flores was more accustomed to it than the Bavaria in which he had spent his youth, and which he now only faintly and rarely recalled. In the telescopic sights of his crossbow, a beautiful multicoloured tropical bird, one of the last of its species, preened itself a quarter of a mile away. De Flores tightened his finger on the trigger. A young man ran from the house.

'Herr De Flores. Herr De Flores.'

De Flores lowered the bow in annoyance. 'What is it, Karl?' he rasped in his usual terse manner. Something in the younger man's face, however, caught his attention.

'Wonderful news,' Karl replied.

2

Only when they were certain that the two large men who had just tried to assassinate them had gone did the Doctor and Ace pull themselves to the river bank. 'Welcome home,' said the Doctor as he hauled Ace out of the water. 'I always liked the Eighties. They were a time of great certainty in England.' While Ace stood drying herself outside the TARDIS, the Doctor went into it and then emerged carrying her ghetto blaster. He had built it for her from a combination of old valves and future technology.

Ace was touched. 'Great,' she said. 'I'll put on my tape from the gig.'

The Doctor fiddled with the controls. 'Not at the moment, Ace.'

'Why not? It's my tape deck.'

'It isn't just a tape deck. And we've got more important things to worry about than your tape. Like people trying to kill us.'

'Who were they? Who'd want to kill us?'

'For me I'm afraid the possibilities are almost infinite,' admitted the Doctor. 'At the moment I'm more concerned about the alarm. Perhaps if I can find out where we're supposed to be going I'll know why it went off.'

A glowing spherical hologram began to form above a dish fitted on the top of the tape deck. As the Doctor adjusted the controls, the image resolved into a computer graphics diagram of a planetary system. This faded, to be replaced by a second diagram.

Ace towelled her hair vigorously. 'Can't be soon enough for me,' she said.

The Doctor was absorbed and replied absently. 'Obviously these arrangements were made in a hurry. It's important though. I've given it a terminal rating.'

'Sounds nice.'

'Oh yes? It means some planet somewhere faces imminent destruction.'

As he spoke, the diagram was replaced by another image. It was clearly a planet.

'Ah,' said the Doctor. 'Now this looks familiar.'

'It should,' said Ace. 'It's the Earth.'

They looked at each other.

The elderly mathematician's scrolls were now yellow with age. Three hundred and fifty years had stiffened them, and the calculations were in parts faded and illegible. The essential information, however, was clear.

The young men stood in respectful silence around the table on which the scrolls lay as De Flores examined them closely, squinting and holding the small figures up to the bright sunlight. The portrait of Hitler which dominated the room seemed suddenly to be caught by the light too, and its expression appeared even more intense than usual. The faintest smile twitched at De Flores' thin mouth. He laid the document down on the table. His voice shook slightly. 'Thank you, Karl. You have done well.'

'I thought you should know at once.'

De Flores looked around the group of young South American men, taking in all their faces. 'Gentlemen,' he said, 'I wonder if even you can fully appreciate what this moment means? You now stand at the turning point of history. The day of fulfilment of our mighty destiny is about to dawn.' His voice seemed to echo and grow louder in the room. 'Fifty years ago I stood at the side of the Führer when he ordered the first giant step to greatness. Just as now the moment approaches for the second, and final one. It will be decisive!'

He turned to the painting behind him and gazed up at it; the young men's eyes followed his. Hitler glared down at them all. De Flores' voice dropped. 'This time,' he added, 'we shall not fail.'

Beneath the portrait a curtain hung to the ground. De Flores crossed to it and drew the curtain aside to reveal a glass case. Inside, a raised dais supported a majestic purple cushion, on top of which lay a silver bow. De Flores gazed at the bow for a moment, then slowly turned to the group again. 'Gentlemen, I give you . . . the Fourth Reich.'

Cheering broke out. In the adjoining room, the telephone rang. Karl hurried out. Smiling, De Flores opened the case and removed the bow reverently. He held it up before them, then placed it in a flight case

18

which he closed and locked. Karl returned. 'Herr De Flores. The aircraft is ready.'

'We leave at once,' replied his leader.

On the pleasant river bank on the other side of the world it was still an idyllic English afternoon. Ace, however, had lost interest in the weather. Even the attempt of less than an hour before on her life and the Doctor's had receded from her mind in the face of more pressing concerns. 'You mean,' she insisted, 'the world's going to end and you'd forgotten?'

'I've been busy,' said the Doctor defensively. 'One thing and another . . .'

As usual, Ace was determined to get to the heart of the matter. 'How long have you known?'

The Doctor squirmed a bit. 'In strictly linear terms, as the chronometer flies . . .' Ace, he could tell, was not going to be blinded by science. He took a deep breath. 'I've known since November the twenty-third, 1638.'

Stepping over the elderly mathematician's body, Richard handed Lady Peinforte a beaker of the fermenting brew that had simmered for the past few days on the fire, and to which he had now added the final ingredient of human blood, reluctantly supplied by the now late scholar. Richard secretly hoped that none of the human hand, an ingredient about which her ladyship had been most insistent, had flaked off into his own beaker. Joining her now in the circle at the centre of the pentacle inscribed on the floor, he felt the unnatural chill from her body and realized he had never stood so physically close to her before. The bright silver arrow she held sparkled unusually in the firelight of the darkened room.

Lady Peinforte glared at him. 'What meanst thou, afraid?' she demanded. 'When I hired you, you led me to believe you were a hardened criminal.'

Richard inclined his head modestly. 'As my lady knows, before I entered your employment I had been found guilty of a large number of offences.'

'Then,' she concluded, 'have the courage of your convictions. Drink.'

Richard looked into the foaming beaker. His courage, seldom if ever adequate, failed him completely.

'*Drink*!'

Faced with the inevitable, Richard closed his eyes and downed the potion. Once he had done so, Lady Peinforte swallowed her own, savouring it slightly with satisfaction. There was a pause, during which Richard's fears abated. Suddenly the arrow in Lady Peinforte's hand began to glow more strongly. It intensified more and more, until the strange silver light seemed to fill the room. Richard was dazzled.

'My lady . . . what is happening?'

Despite the increasing brightness, Lady Peinforte's eyes were even more visible. They now seemed to Richard to have become the only recognizable points in a blinding universe. Around them the colours of the room were spinning and mixing. Richard felt himself hurtling down an endless dark tunnel filled with voices, all passing much too fast to make sense . . . and yet she was still there beside him, staring through him, crushing his meagre will with her own.

Somewhere at the centre of the heavens through which they now seemed to be rushing at unimaginable speed, the arrow was shining with a brightness that Richard had never thought possible. Yet throughout, very dimly, he was aware of the door that led to the world outside, to the streets of Windsor where he had spent all his life, to everyone he knew. If he could only reach the door they would all be there as usual, waiting . . .

With more effort than he had ever made before at anything, Richard screamed: 'Noooo . . .' He broke free and stepped out of the circle, desperately reaching for the door.

Lady Peinforte howled at him above the thousands of voices rushing though his brain. 'Come back, you fool, you will break the aura.'

Richard fell to his knees, panic-stricken. Now he knew how madmen felt, whom he with the rest had paid to watch and prod. Oh, never, never again. 'I can't,' he pleaded. 'Please, my lady. I must stay.'

'It's too late.' Reaching out, she dragged him back into the pentacle. Richard whimpered with terror. Suddenly he was no longer separate from the insanity of sound and light around him but part of it. He no longer existed as a being separate from anything else. He was a fraction of everything; everything that ever had been, or was, or would be and all of it rushing madly forward to its oblivion.

Slowly, stillness returned; the blur of sight and sound was restored little by little to reality. Lady Peinforte looked around in approval. Richard, by contrast, was extremely nervous. A sudden passing roar outside shook him badly.

21

'Where . . . where are we my lady?' he whispered.

Lady Peinforte replied at her usual bold volume. 'The very place we left, of course. My house in Windsor. Much improved too.

Richard looked doubtfully at the sign he was unable to read in the window, which advertised the premises as the Princess of Wales Burger Bar. 'What's happened to it?' he asked.

'History, Richard,' said Lady Peinforte, briskly. 'Progress. It is the year of our Lord nineteen eighty-eight.'

Further explanation was prevented as the room filled, once again, with dazzling silver light. The prospect of another journey through time filled Richard with immediate terror. 'Gracious heaven, my lady. What's that?'

Lady Peinforte was already at the window, an expression of dreamy wonder suffusing her hard features.

'The mathematician was right,' she answered distantly. 'She is returning. Look!'

Outside, the streetlit gloom of Windsor High Street was bathed in silver luminescence.

Only a few hundred yards away, yet unseen by anyone, the TARDIS materialized. The windowless vaults in which it appeared were dimly lit at night, and at first Ace was uncertain that she was seeing a large number of glass cases containing treasures of many kinds. The Doctor had already rushed ahead: he examined each case quickly, then hurried on to the next.

'Wow!' said Ace. 'Look at all this stuff.'

'That's exactly what we've got to do,' replied the Doctor. 'You start over there.'

Ace was mystified. 'What's it all for?'

'They're presents.' The Doctor paused briefly in front of a Maori tribal head-dress and bustled on.

'Nobody gets this many presents.'

The Doctor paused momentarily. 'If you were a lady who did a lot of travelling . . .' he began.

'I am,' said Ace.

'But we're not always invited are we? If we were, you'd probably be given presents wherever you went. And you'd have to keep them somewhere.'

Ace peered at a jewelled tiara. 'Who does it all belong to?' she continued. 'I never heard of anywhere like this in . . .'

'Windsor,' the Doctor supplied.

'Windsor?' said Ace. The penny dropped. 'We're in the castle.'

The Doctor stopped at another case. 'I say. That's new.'

Ace took in the windowless dark chamber more fully. 'I thought it'd be a lot posher than this,' she said.

'It probably is upstairs. But we're in the vaults. And somewhere in here is a very beautiful silver bow, which we are going to borrow and look after.'

Ace was horrified. 'We can't go nicking stuff from here.'

'It's purely temporary,' assured the Doctor from the front of another display case.

23

'It's probably treason. I'm too young to go to the Tower.'

The Doctor stopped. He was very serious. 'Ace, would it make any difference if I remind you that the safety of the entire world depends on it?'

'It'd make a difference if you'd tell me what's going on, Professor.' She saw the look in his face and continued before he had a chance to reply. 'But I suppose there's no time to explain now.'

'Precisely,' said the Doctor. Suddenly, the already dim electric light flickered sharply, then righted itself. 'Perhaps even less than I thought.'

Outside the Princess of Wales Burger Bar, the night was filled with dazzling silver luminescence and a gale-force wind. The silver arrow in Lady Peinforte's hand was growing brighter by the moment. Lady Peinforte gazed rapturously at the sky. 'Nemesis!' she cried above the wind. 'She arrives.'

At that moment, a meteor with four tails of fire behind it flashed out of the silver darkness above them and hurtled to the Earth, disappearing behind the buildings opposite. There was what sounded like a very loud explosion which shook the ground and buildings throughout the town, then silence.

The Doctor caught a Ming vase which had toppled from its vibrating stand. He replaced it carefully but did not speak.

'Was that a bomb?' asked Ace.

The Doctor's face was worryingly serious. 'That,' he replied, making quite certain the vase was in the correct spot, 'was the return to Earth of a meteor called the Nemesis which has been in orbit for exactly three hundred and fifty years.'

Ace was impressed. 'You really are amazing, Professor,' she said, 'telling all that from just the noise.'

The Doctor looked at her sadly. 'It's not difficult really. It was me who fired it into space.' He looked away. His voice raised suddenly. 'I think this may qualify as the worst miscalculation ever committed in the entire dimensional reaches of space and time.'

Ace desperately searched for something to say. 'Anyone can make a mistake,' she tried brightly.

Beyond him, she noticed something. 'Look,' she said excitedly. 'There's the bow.'

They hurried wordlessly to a large glass case. Reaching it, however, they realized immediately that it contained nothing except a bow-shaped space. Above the case was a notice.

As the large van swung into the M4 exit for Windsor, Karl snatched a glance at De Flores. The older man was wide-awake, staring into the flight case which had not left his hands during the entire journey from South America. The lid was open, and the silver bow glowed softly in the darkness, creating the illusion that his face had been covered in silver. Behind them, the armed young men dozed.

'There,' said the Doctor, 'it was.'

Ace shone her torch and read the notice aloud. 'This case contained the Bow of Nemesis, property of the Crown, which disappeared mysteriously in 1788. Legend has it that unless a place is kept for the bow in the castle, the entire silver statue will return to destroy the world.'

The Doctor gazed dejectedly at the empty case. 'For once, legend is entirely correct. It has just come back.'

For a second time, the already dim electric lights flickered noticeably for a moment, then returned to normal. 'And now this,' he added bitterly.

'It's just the electricity,' said Ace. 'It does that sometimes, even in 1988. What I want to know is, how can a statue destroy the world?'

The Doctor, however, was already hurrying towards the TARDIS. Ace followed. 'No time?' she asked.

The Doctor activated the door, which opened obediently. 'I'll tell you three hundred and fifty years ago,' he promised.

The candles were almost burnt out now and the already dark room was even more gloomy. The remains of the fire provided such light as there was. The TARDIS materialized just outside the pentacle. The Doctor and Ace crept into the room.

'Ssh,' whispered the Doctor. 'We don't know who's at home.'

Ace whispered back firmly. 'We've got a deal, Professor,' she reminded him.

'We're in Windsor, of course,' whispered the Doctor impatiently. 'A few hundred yards from the castle.' He was already busy, searching among the shadows of the room. Ace looked around nervously and shuddered involuntarily. There was an atmosphere of evil about the room and, she decided, about the house as a whole. She followed the Doctor.

'And it really is 1638?' she asked.

'It certainly is,' replied the Doctor briskly. 'And furthermore . . . *don't move!*'

Ace froze. She peered through the darkness, straining to see what had so shocked the Doctor. 'Don't come any nearer,' he hissed, before she could ask.

He moved forward. Behind a chair, the elderly mathematician's body lay in a wide puddle of congealing blood. The whites of his eyes stared dully up at them. Ace caught her breath.

'Whose house is this?' she heard herself ask.

The Doctor was kneeling to examine the body. 'A lady's,' he replied grimly.

'She's got funny ideas about home furnishing,' said Ace in disgust. She turned away and opened the window. The night was a velvet curtain and the air was the freshest she had ever breathed. She felt a little better.

'Lady Peinforte's nothing if not original,' continued the Doctor. He picked up a scroll of calculation and examined it carefully. 'But I'm afraid this poor man was employed for his useful rather than ornamental qualities. He was a scholar.' Pulling out his abacus, he made a rapid series of calculations, checking the figures on the scroll against his own conclusions. He returned the abacus to his pocket thoughtfully. 'He's done remarkably well too,' he added. 'In a matter of months since I left here, he's worked out the exact date and time when the meteor known as the Nemesis will return. November the twenty-third . . .'

'1988,' supplied Ace.

'And Lady Peinforte has rewarded him with her usual generosity.' The Doctor covered the mathematician's face with a cloth and stood up.

'So the bow belonged to her?'

'To a statue of her. She had it made from some silver metal which fell from the sky into the meadow out there.'

There was a sudden creak from the corner of the room. Ace jumped. The Doctor smiled bitterly. 'It's all right. There's no one here now apart from our late friend. Lady Peinforte will be in Windsor all right, but three hundred and fifty years in the future.'

Ace was surprised. 'How can she get to 1988?'

It was clear that the Doctor's mind was occupied with distant problems. He spoke absently, staring at the fire. 'She'll have used the arrow, of course. She had certain rudimentary ideas about time travel – black magic mostly – as well as what might be called a nose for secrets.'

'So it wasn't silver, this stuff that fell out of the sky?'

The Doctor snorted with something that was almost laughter. 'Unfortunately, Lady Peinforte discovered it was something rather more unusual: the living metal validium.'

Ace looked blank.

'The most dangerous substance in existence.'

* * *

28

Three hundred and fifty years in the future, although, as the Doctor rightly surmised, only a few hundred yards away, the arrow glowed dully in Lady Peinforte's hand as she wrapped it in a towel from behind the counter of the Princess of Wales Burger Bar. Richard struggled with the baffling complexity of the Yale lock on the door. Latches had evidently grown more complex since his time, he thought. Lady Peinforte was, as usual, impatient.

'Now we have but to take the statue,' she said. 'The peasants will be much excited and we can pass among them unnoticed and find our opportunity to seize it. Hurry, there's no time to lose.'

The door, however, refused to yield. Outside there was another of the roars which had disturbed Richard previously. He watched in wonder as a police car sped past, its blue light flashing on the roof. Sensing its purpose, Lady Peinforte could wait no longer. 'Hurry!' she yelled. 'The rogue will have the Nemesis.'

The lock, however, still refused to move. 'I have not seen the like of it, my lady,' Richard admitted nervously.

Lady Peinforte gave a screech of frustration. 'Am I to be a prisoner in my own house while world dominion waits beyond the door?' she screamed. 'I'd have got married if I'd wanted that.'

Richard was secretly not altogether unhappy that they were, at least temporarily, forced to remain in the relative safety of the building. Who could tell how many more of the roaring carriages there were outside? 'Such light without fire,' he breathed. 'And the noise. We must take care, my lady.'

'Fie!' Lady Peinforte picked up a plastic child's chair and hurled it through the window, shattering the garish lettering which read 'Come right in!' Immediately the continuous electric bell of the burglar alarm tore into the quiet of the night. Lady Peinforte and Richard stared at each other open-mouthed. Lady Peinforte was the first to recover. She leapt through the shattered window into the street outside. Terrified, Richard followed.

Down the strange-scented street they ran, headlong into the twentieth century. Rounding a corner they saw the police car, now motionless, and a man standing next to it looking through a wire fence into what seemed to be a partly completed metal building. Lady Peinforte and Richard ducked into a doorway and watched the man carefully. He had not seen them.

'What means yon blue fellow?' whispered Richard. 'Why speaks he to his hand?'

Lady Peinforte was again instinctive about the activities of the police. 'He summons guards,' she said angrily. 'Oh, this cannot be.' There was silence for a moment, disturbed only by the distant crackle of traffic on the policeman's radio as his call was answered.

'Why so upset, my lady?' said Richard.

Lady Peinforte flared. 'Must I always be surrounded by fools?' she cried, loudly enough to give Richard palpitations. 'Because, fool, they will protect the Nemesis, and we know not their strength and weapons.'

'But, my lady,' Richard spoke gently, 'they know

not what the comet is. And without the arrow it is nothing. We have but to watch and wait our chance to seize it.'

There was a pause as this sank in. Lady Peinforte turned to him, considering. 'Thou art not in all wise so useless, Richard.'

Richard bowed. 'My lady is too kind.'

Lady Peinforte became decisive once again. 'We'll go outside the town and hide until morning.'

Crossing in front of the statue of Queen Victoria, they made their way past the railway station and towards open country.

In a street on the opposite side of the building site in which the meteor had come to ground, the van was stationary outside a multi-storey car park. In the passenger seat, the glowing bow illuminated the outside of the flight case, even though it was locked inside. De Flores gazed raptly at the site. 'In the new era,' his voice trembled with emotion, 'this place will be a shrine.'

Karl waited diplomatically, but presumed to speak when no more was forthcoming. 'We await only your order,' he said politely. De Flores smiled gently at him.

'Good!' he replied. He settled back comfortably. 'Then let us drive to the best hotel and enjoy a good night's sleep.'

Behind him the young paramilitaries looked at each other in astonishment. De Flores glanced round, and smiled indulgently. 'You young people,' he admonished. 'Always in such a hurry. Well, we were the same. The statue is inside a meteor which has just travelled through space. Have you any idea how hot it will be? How can we handle it yet? Because the British Government is completely unaware of its power, I am sure we can rely on the police force to guard it safely until morning, when it will be ready for us to collect. I have every confidence in them.' He turned forward again, and snapped his fingers. 'The hotel.'

Lady Peinforte and Richard were less comfortably accommodated among some bushes in the park, although Richard alone seemed aware of the rumble of approaching thunder: her ladyship was absorbed in more important thoughts. Richard slowly turned the rabbit he was roasting over the fire. 'I am in a nightmare,' he said to himself, 'or mad.'

Lady Peinforte was jolted into reality by his voice. 'This is no madness. It is England. Pull yourself together,' she snapped.

'But the noise, my lady. The foul air . . .' A further look from Lady Peinforte was enough. Richard subsided unhappily. 'Yes, my lady.' There was a silence. Richard searched his imagination for some means of placating her. 'What will my lady do when you possess the Nemesis?'

For the first time, something akin to warmth crossed Lady Peinforte's face. 'Do?' she said. 'Why, have revenge, first and last. First on that predictable little man who thought he could thwart me. He will soon arrive, Richard.' Richard stared at her in disbelief. Not for the first time, her ladyship's foreknowledge startled him. Lady Peinforte smiled, enjoying the effect. 'Oh yes,' she continued. 'I expect him. And this time there'll be a reckoning with the nameless Doctor whose power is so secret. *For I have found out his secret.*' Her voice was rising uncontrollably. There was a sudden flash of lightning, illuminating her face in sudden and brilliant silver light. A great rolling crash of thunder seemed to split the sky in two, releasing a torrential downpour. Lady Peinforte continued unheeding, her entire being animated by hatred. 'In good time I shall speak it. I shall be his downfall.'

The three policemen who climbed from their car to investigate and guard the crashed meteor, as De Flores rightly predicted, had approached it without great interest. It was only when the first, shining his torch on the smoking lump of rock now embedded into the ground near the half-completed building, had called several times to the other two in the car that a second got out to take a look. In the light of both their torches, and in mounting disbelief, they confirmed what the first thought he had seen. A woman's face, cast in silver, was clearly visible through a glass panel set in the rock. It stared back at them blankly through the rain.

It was at this moment that the car's engine, which had been left running, suddenly cut out with a strange grinding sound. It was as if the battery had suddenly and completely lost all its power. The driver, still in his seat, tried to restart the car, but discovered it was completely dead. He released the bonnet and, climbing out, opened it and began without success to try to identify the fault.

The first policeman reached for his radio and had given his call sign before he noticed that it, too, was completely inoperative. Its power had apparently evaporated instantly. He shook it and tried again. His companion discovered that his radio was in precisely the same condition.

Occupied as they now all were by these mysterious failures, they did not notice the group of thin silver pipes which rose from the ground near them. Even had they done so, the gas that the pipes began to release into the air was invisible. The policemen immediately fell unconscious.

The silver face stared dimly out through its glass panel into the rain and the now silent darkness.

3

There was an outburst of clicks and whirrs from the cameras of the enthusiastic party of Japanese tourists on the North Terrace of Windsor Castle. The guide stood back smiling and glanced surreptitiously at her watch as the private after-dinner walk of Elizabeth the First was devoured by the cameras, which then turned equal attention to the magnificent view beyond. The roof of Eton College Chapel glowed gold even at quarter to ten in the grey morning.

Such was the visitors' interest that the materialization of the TARDIS a few yards away passed unnoticed. The Doctor and Ace stepped out. Ace sniffed the damp air as she looked around.

'I've been here before,' she announced.

'Déjà vu?' enquired the Doctor, interested. He had never been able to decide whether he considered it a phenomenon or an illusion.

'No,' said Ace, 'with the school.'

The Doctor was cheered by this. 'Oh good,' he said, 'I've not been since they were building the place. You'll be able to remember the way round.'

'Not really.' Ace looked worried. 'Windsor Castle is a big place.'

'Quite right,' agreed the Doctor. 'What we need is a guide. Come on.'

The tour guide had by now marshalled the party, and led the way into the castle building, where the last of them were disappearing. The Doctor and Ace joined the back of the group and looked up with interest, as the rest were doing, at the ceiling as they passed into the building.

Their inability to speak Japanese, coupled with the guide's soft vocal delivery, hindered the pair's enjoyment of the finer points of the tour. The disappointment, however, was short-lived: within a minute the Doctor was tugging at Ace's sleeve. 'This way,' he muttered. He nodded towards a door marked 'No Entry'. Before Ace could react he was trying the handle: the door opened. The party began moving towards the next point of interest. Ace followed the Doctor through the door, which he closed softly behind them.

They found themselves in a dark corridor. The Doctor was already hurrying ahead. Catching up with him, Ace decided to voice her misgivings. 'I really don't think we should be doing this,' she tried. It was without effect. They reached a crossroads between three corridors. The Doctor paused and looked about, clearly trying to get his bearings.

'What do you think,' he asked at his normal forthright volume. 'This way?'

'I might be able to say if I knew where we were going,' Ace whispered. 'But we didn't actually cover the royal residential areas on the school trip.'

The Doctor, having made a decision, was already

marching away in another direction. Ace, following, glimpsed a movement in the distance. She caught up with the Doctor and took his arm, warningly. She whispered loudly in his ear: 'There's someone coming.'

The Doctor was undeterred. 'Look as if you own the place,' he answered.'

'Do what?'

'Never fails.' He sailed on down the corridor, full of confidence. Ace tood a deep breath and followed.

As the figure neared, Ace's reservations increased massively, turning to a sudden certainty of recognition. 'Doctor!' she said, urgently. The Doctor, however, continued. Ace pulled him into a doorway. 'We own the place,' he repeated.

Ace pointed silently at the woman approaching. It could now be seen that she was accompanied by a number of small dogs.

'How annoying,' said the Doctor. 'I can't place her for the life of me.'

Ace put her hand over his mouth to prevent any further sound as the Queen passed within a yard of them, a number of corgis playing around her feet. The Doctor struggled but Ace kept hold of him until the sound of the royal footsteps had faded, when the Doctor struggled free.

'It's all right, Ace,' he said, desperately, keeping well clear of her. 'I know her from somewhere.'

'Of course you do,' said Ace.

A second later the ancient stones of the castle were rent by an anguished cry.

'Whaaat?' shouted the Doctor 'Why didn't you say something?'

'You wouldn't let me,' replied Ace, reasonably.

'Her Majesty the Queen's exactly who we need,' the Doctor yelled. 'Quick! after her.'

He bolted down the corridor after the Queen. Ace, naturally, followed.

Within seconds they arrived at a junction of other corridors. The Doctor stopped, lunged in one direction, thought better of it, and stopped again. He lunged in another, and stopped again. The ancient stone walls seemed to reflect his blankness mockingly. As Ace caught up with him, he noticed a third option. Immediately next to him was a door. On the door was the imprint of a golden crown. The Doctor beamed at Ace in triumph. 'Aha,' he cried, reaching for the doorknob. Ace's hand flashed forward and grabbed his.

'We can't go in there,' she said desperately.

The Doctor was firm. 'Don't you think it would be very useful to have the police, not to mention the armed services, on our side? Of course it would. And who better to go to for help in mobilizing them than their commander-in-chief? Cut through all the red tape.'

'Hold on, Doctor,' said Ace weakly.

But the Doctor was deady serious. 'There really is no alternative, believe me,' he said. 'The worst people the world has to offer will be on their way to Windsor right now.' He raised his hand to knock authoritatively. Another hand seized his. It was immensely strong. Ace and the Doctor turned to discover two large fit-looking men in suits, one of whom was the owner of the hand. He lowered the Doctor's arm slowly. Ace realized they clearly meant business.

'What are you doing here?' he asked.

'I can't possibly discuss that with you,' replied the Doctor firmly, drawing himself up to his full height. This brought him impressively level with the man's chest. 'Who, may I ask, are you?'

'Palace security,' replied the second man, who was if anything larger than the first.

'Oh good.' The Doctor warmed at once. 'I have to speak to Her Majesty.'

'You were right,' said the first security man to the second one. 'Mental.' He turned back to the Doctor. 'Don't worry,' he said in the louder than usual tone that the English reserve for foreigners and the ill. 'We'll have a doctor here soon.'

For once, thought Ace, it was really a good thing the Doctor had two hearts. One would not be enough to sustain the immediate rise in blood pressure which erupted inside him.

'I *am* the Doctor,' he shouted at the top of his voice.

'Don't get excited,' warned the first security man. 'How did you get in here?'

'I can tell you now that you won't believe me,' answered the Doctor haughtily.

The first security man spoke patiently, as if to an angry child: 'Try us.'

The Doctor glared at him in defiance. 'I travelled through space and time,' he said. He looked evenly at both of them.

'Dear, oh dear,' said the first security man to the second, who rolled his eyes.

'See?' howled the Doctor. 'What did I tell you? Very well, in that case I demand you escort us to Her Majesty at once.'

To the Doctor's apparent surprise, however, the first security man completely ignored him and turned to Ace. 'Are you a patient with him?' he asked.

Ace was extremely angry at seeing the Doctor treated with such disrespect. She glared at the large man. 'You'd better listen to him, weasel features. He's the Doctor,' she insisted.

The first security man nodded sagely. 'Oh, is he?' he said patiently. He glanced significantly at his companion.

The Doctor sighed. 'No,' he said, and gestured down the corridor behind the two men. 'He's the Doctor.' There was a second's pause. The security men did not even flicker towards looking over their shoulders. The first smiled sadly and shook his head. 'Don't try that one with us,' he said.

The Doctor appeared to give in. 'Oh, all right,' he agreed. 'How about this?' Suddenly a look of peculiar intensity came over his eyes, a look which Ace had never seen before. Suddenly his voice became fascinating, seeming to summon all their concentration into his power. 'The fate of every living creature on this planet hangs in the balance,' said the Doctor distinctly.

There was a moment's silence. The security men shook their heads as if to clear them. Despite themselves, the men were shaken. 'I don't believe you,' said the first hesitantly. Ace, however, was aware that neither of the two men could not remove his eyes from the Doctor's. His voice, controlling them, had become low and hypnotic. 'You will believe me,' the Doctor continued, staring into their eyes, which were becoming dormant. 'You will let us go. You will not move.' The two security men were as if rooted where they stood, staring blankly forward. The Doctor took Ace's arm and began to lead her quietly away.

'How did you do that?' she whispered, once they were a few yards down the corridor.

The Doctor, seldom a patron of false modesty, smiled complacently. 'Oh, it's quite easy really,' he said. There was a sudden cry from behind them. Looking back, Ace saw the two security men break into a run after them. 'The only trouble is,' the Doctor continued, taking Ace's arm and breaking into a dash himself, 'it doesn't last very long.' They bolted down the corridor, pursued by the two security men.

Rounding a corner breathlessly, they hesitated for a moment. A large double door was ahead of them. They hurtled through it.

There was what seemed to Ace after the gloom of the corridor a blaze of light, crowded with smiling oriental faces as she and the Doctor charged through the centre of the group of Japanese tourists in whose company they had entered the castle, apologizing profusely as they shouldered the visitors aside. In the background, the security men burst through the door and headed full pelt for the centre of the disarrayed but reassembling group of tourists. The Doctor and Ace fled through the opposite exit and into a larger, brighter corridor. Ahead of them was a wide and magnificent flight of stairs lined with paintings. They charged down it. At the bottom was a recess, into which they crammed themselves and began to regain their breath.

'What now?' panted Ace.

'Back to the TARDIS,' replied the Doctor. 'We must get the statue before anyone else does, and we're obviously not going to get any help here.' He moved to leave. Stepping forward to follow him, Ace's attention was caught by one of the pictures. She halted. 'Professor!' she called. The Doctor stopped.

'What now?' he asked, glancing back up the stairs, where at any moment he expected the security men to appear. Ace pointed at the painting. It showed a rich young woman in eighteenth century dress: the green countryside rolling away in the eternal background, her eyes perfectly certain that its ownership would lie unchanged in the hands of her descendants forever.

Ace's expression was one of wonder. 'That's me,' she said.

'What?' The Doctor stepped closer and examined it. Recognition dawned. 'Oh yes. Not a bad likeness was it?' He began to walk away. Ace was staggered.

'But . . .' she began.

The Doctor smiled indulgently and patted her on the arm. 'It's all right,' he said in a comforting tone. 'It hasn't happened yet.'

Ace looked at him blankly. 'But that was painted two hundred years ago.'

The Doctor smiled patiently. 'I know,' he replied, 'but we haven't done it yet. That's why you can't remember.'

Ace struggled for a moment to work out the Doctor's logic. She was still mystified. 'That doesn't make sense,' she finally said.

The Doctor sighed the sigh of a being forever misunderstood. 'It did to Louis Armstrong,' he murmured sadly. 'He really understood time.'

4

At the building site, everything was still. The three policemen lay where they had collapsed, breathing but unconscious.

Suddenly and simultaneously through each of the windows, De Flores' armed paramilitaries burst in. Fanning out across the site they quickly and expertly searched every square foot before assuming defensive positions. It was only then that De Flores arrived, impatient though he clearly was. He carried the flight case in which he had placed the bow, and was already gazing intently at the smoking hole into which the comet had made its landfall. Karl awaited him, a puzzled look on his face.

'Herr De Flores, I don't understand how the police have already been overcome.'

De Flores brushed this aside and hurried towards the comet. 'That is of no importance,' he replied. 'All that matters is that the Nemesis is safe.' He gazed down at the smouldering ball of rock. The silver face seemed to stare back blankly at him, partly visible through the glass panel. De Flores stepped forward and tenderly wiped away some mud from it with his handkerchief. He stared into its eyes, a look of adoration suffusing his hard features. 'At last,' he said, addressing the statue. 'I know why you have come. Your long journey is over. I alone understand you, and I have brought what you need.'

Reverently, he unlocked the flight case and flipped open the lid. Inside lay the silver bow. For a moment, nothing happened. Then through the rock there was a spasm of luminescence like a sudden flash of lightning on a summer night. For a brief instant, the statue of a woman was clearly visible through the rock and mud. The darkness which followed was absolute, as though light had never existed. Almost immediately there was a second spasm of the dazzling silver light inside the rock, this time even brighter and longer. The silver light picked out the rapt watching face of De Flores and the faces of the young men around him, their expressions caught for an instant half-way between terror and fascination. More spasms followed, building in intensity until the rock was pulsating with light. There was a deafening crack that sounded like thunder, and the rock split in two, its two halves edged with fire as they fell away. The silver woman's form lay revealed, emanating silver light so sharp it was almost blinding. The young men shielded their eyes. De Flores, however, seemed to thrive on the power he had unleashed and stood firm, appearing to breathe in strength from the very presence of the Nemesis.

'Your strength returns,' he whispered. 'Soon you will be completely restored.' His voice suddenly rose. 'But . . .' He stepped forward and knocked away the last of the rock casing which covered the statue's left hand. He was horrified. Suddenly frantic, he turned to the others. 'Where is the arrow?'

The young men looked at one another, incomprehensibly.

'It must be here,' screamed De Flores, scrabbling wildly in the mud. 'Find it. *Find it!*'

Instantly obedient, they began examining the ground around the comet. Deeply involved in their search, they were unaware of the TARDIS materializing a few yards away, and of the Doctor and Ace stepping out.

'I do hope we're not too late,' yelled the Doctor over his shoulder as he rushed forward. Turning to face the way he was going, he pulled up immediately, but it was too late. They were staring down the barrels of eight high-velocity weapons. The Doctor was reassuring. Lifting his hat with a polite smile he addressed the young men in his best diplomatic manner. 'Don't worry. We're not going to hurt you.'

Karl was shaken. 'How did you get here?' he demanded. He turned to De Flores. 'I searched that section. There was no one there.'

De Flores had risen to his feet. 'Never mind, Karl,' he said impatiently. 'You will see many signs and wonders in the days to come. We have only one concern with these . . . conjurers.' He faced the Doctor. 'Give me the arrow of Nemesis.'

The Doctor, however, was perfectly composed. 'Fortunately,' he replied, 'I haven't seen it since 1638 when it disappeared with the good Lady Peinforte.'

'Rubbish.' De Flores turned to Ace, who shivered

involuntarily. 'You. This is your only chance to save yourself. Where is the arrow?'

'I know nothing about it,' said Ace. The Doctor stepped forward protectively.

'She really doesn't,' he told De Flores. 'Allow me to explain, Ace.' Turning his back on the guns of the paramilitaries and on De Flores he proceeded to do so with his customary animation. 'You see, for validium to become active you must have a sufficient quantity of it. A critical mass, in fact. The statue alone is not enough without the bow . . .'

'I have the bow,' De Flores interrupted emphatically.

'And,' continued the Doctor, ignoring him, 'the arrow. But if someone could put the bow and the arrow into the statue's hands . . .'

'They have the power of life and death, not only over the Earth but over any planet in existence.' De Flores completed the explanation for him. There was silence. The German stared menacingly at the pair. His voice became sinister. 'You are,' he said slowly, 'remarkably well informed for someone who claims to know nothing.'

The Doctor looked at him, unequivocally. 'I simply notice what is obvious. You apparently don't.'

'What do you mean?' demanded Karl. Ace realized from his tone that Karl was rattled.

The Doctor pressed home his moment of advantage. 'Can you smell anything?' he asked, sharply. The paramilitaries looked at one another. Even De Flores sniffed.

'Building materials,' he responded.

The Doctor smiled drily. 'Nerve gas,' he said. His face became steely. 'Oh, you're forgiven. This is of a kind with which you would be entirely unfamiliar.'

De Flores suddenly lost his temper. 'Who are you?' he demanded, savagely. The Doctor, however, was in full flow.

'Doesn't it occur to you to wonder what happened to these policemen?' he continued.

'I asked that,' said Karl eagerly. The Doctor smiled indulgently. 'Well done,' he said with approval, kneeling to examine one of the unconscious figures on the ground. 'And what, I wonder,' he said distantly as he did so, 'were your conclusions?'

'Don't play games with us.' De Flores's voice was deadly.

'I haven't the time.' The Doctor stood up. Suddenly, he too was utterly serious. 'These men have been attacked by a technology more advanced and more terrible than you can imagine.'

Karl struggled with disbelief. 'What technology?' he asked. But De Flores cut in sharply.

'That's quite enough nonsense,' he said.

'And look at their cars,' continued the Doctor, ignoring him. 'Look at their radios. Isn't it strange they all seem to have failed at once?'

Karl was unable to disguise his fascination. 'I thought that too,' he said.

'Very good,' replied the Doctor, with the faintest hint of sarcasm. 'Clearly their batteries are no longer operative. You might also have noticed one or two hiccups in the local electricity supply during the last few days.'

'Like at the castle?' Despite the danger of their situation, Ace too was unable to resist the lure of the mystery to which the Doctor evidently knew the answer.

'Exactly,' he confirmed. He looked around at his audience in satisfaction. De Flores, however, had reached the limit of his patience.

'Tell me where the arrow is,' he shouted.

'Listen,' replied the Doctor 'and you might just save your life. There are creatures in the universe which make you look as dangerous as babies. And they're here for the same reason you are.'

De Flores took the gun Karl was holding and raised it. 'You will now tell me,' he said, quietly, 'where to find the arrow.'

'I am very glad to say I can't,' the Doctor replied firmly.

'Then,' concluded De Flores, 'I will shoot her.' He aimed the gun squarely at Ace.

There was a terrible silence. Even the Doctor was still. De Flores began to squeeze the trigger.

Ace murmured: 'Doctor . . .'

Suddenly there was a blinding sheet of light, dazzling them all. As their eyes became accustomed to the glare, they turned to its apparent source, some yards away. De Flores' face turned deadly white; every trace of colour draining from it in his amazement. Ace stood open-mouthed at what she saw. Some twenty yards away, a disc-shaped spacecraft had appeared in silence. A door panel was sliding open. From it, a first, then a second, and a third, silver figure stepped out. They were, Ace reckoned, about

49

eight feet tall. She dimly registered that the paramilitaries, Karl, and De Flores were mesmerized by the spectacle of them. Suddenly she knew she was not going to be shot after all. Shock and relief flooded through her. The Doctor's voice cut into her consciousness; his tone was at its most severely authoritative.

'Don't move,' he hissed.

Ace found her voice with difficulty. 'What . . . what are they?' she whispered, unable to take her eyes from the group of now eight silver figures which, having assembled outside the spacecraft, were beginning to advance towards them with heavy steps. The Doctor's face was twisted in hatred.

'Cybermen,' he answered quietly.

5

The Cyber Leader approached first. Behind and to his left, he was flanked by his Lieutenant. The others spread out behind them. The paramilitaries stared at them aghast.

The Cybermen came to a halt, the Leader's attention directly on the Doctor.

'So, Doctor,' the metallic voice grated. 'A new appearance. Otherwise our anticipation of your presence has proved entirely accurate.'

From the corner of her eye, Ace caught the movement as one of the paramilitaries, apparently unobserved, swung his machine-gun and fired a rapid burst at the Leader. There was no effect. The others immediately followed suit; there was a deafening blast of gunfire as they all opened up at the Cybermen. The bullets bounced off them. The gunfire stopped, the paramilitaries staring in disbelief. Slowly, ponderously, the Cyber Leader turned towards the man who had first shot at him, and raised his laser gun. There was a sudden flash of light from the muzzle, and the man fell dead.

'Cover!' shouted De Flores. The paramilitaries scattered for concealment.

'Eradicate them,' boomed the Cyber Leader.

The Cybermen immediately opened up with lasers, to be met by the automatic fire of the paramilitaries. The noise was continuous and deafening. A steel girder supporting a partly constructed wall dissolved as a laser shaft glanced across it, bringing down the side of a building. The machine-gun bullets, meanwhile, continued to bounce uselessly off the Cybermen.

Through the smoke and dust, Ace glimpsed the Doctor. He was kneeling in the crater where the Nemesis had landed, apparently deep in thought. Taking a careful look round, and discovering the warring factions were fully occupied with each other, she crawled towards him.

'Doctor!' she called. The Doctor, absorbed, did not hear her. Reaching him, she put her hand on his shoulder. He looked up at her in surprise.

'Ah, Ace,' he murmured. 'There you are.'

'Come on,' said Ace, urgently, ducking as a stray burst of bullets whizzed over their heads. 'We can't stay here.'

'We certainly can,' replied the Doctor with some asperity. 'This is exactly what happened last time. The only difference is that then it was Lady Peinforte and agents of the Inquisition. Well that's not going to happen again.'

No sooner had he spoken than Ace noticed a nearby Cyberman stagger and fall as an arrow hit and lodged in his chest panel.

The Doctor's attention, meanwhile, was still largely submerged in his calculations. 'Imagine,' he said testily, 'trying to calculate the correct angle of projection, taking into account gravity and all the rest of it, while all around you people are trying to kill each other. No wonder I got the sums wrong.'

Ace, however, was watching the Cyberman, who was writhing in what was clearly agony. His movements grew slower.

'Utter waste of time shooting at them, of course,' the Doctor continued over his shoulder, rattling his abacus with dexterity as the gunfire and explosions continued unabated. 'As you'll have realized, they're completely bullet-proof.' He giggled slightly. 'Those men might just as well be using bows and arrows.'

Ace smiled grimly. 'It looks like they're a bit more effective,' she said.

The Doctor looked up at her fully for the first time. 'What?' he asked.

On the partly finished roof of a nearby building, Lady Peinforte looked on with satisfaction as the stricken Cyberman's faltering movements grew slower and then stopped. She turned to Richard. 'A hit, a palpable hit, Richard,' she said.

She discovered that Richard, oblivious to her words, was praying on his knees. 'And I shall devote myself to good works,' she heard him murmur. 'Swear will I never, steal not, and observe evermore the Lord's day.'

Lady Peinforte snorted in disgust and reloaded her bow. 'See,' she said rather more loudly, 'how my poison is as deadly as ever, Richard.'

'I shall comfort the sick,' continued Richard. 'Which reminds me, I'll return to Briggs his money.'

Exasperated at his attention to God, which she felt was unquestionably better expended on herself, Lady Peinforte kicked him. Richard yelped and opened his eyes.

'Get up, fool,' she snarled. Richard rose hastily, rubbing himself. Assured he was now listening, Lady Peinforte continued. 'I tell thee,' she said warmly, 'were there men of silver like these in our day, my life had been quite different.' For a moment an unusual, almost dreamy expression, which Richard had never seen there before, crossed her sharp features. It vanished as quickly as it had appeared, to be replaced by her normal calculating sneer. 'Now, though, I'll let them all destroy each other, then we take the Nemesis.' She pulled back the bowstring and fired another arrow into the mêlée below.

Seventy-five feet away, another Cyberman fell. Crouched under cover near him, De Flores watched as Lady Peinforte's arrow proved as deadly as the last. His men were falling right and left, and it was clear that soon he and Karl, who was providing pointless covering fire from next to him, would be the last left. He shook Karl's shoulder. The young man stopped firing and cocked his ear to De Flores.

'We must retreat,' shouted De Flores above the gunfire. 'It's our only chance of final victory.'

Karl was disbelieving. 'And leave the statue?' he shouted back. To his surprise, De Flores agreed.

'The statue alone is useless to them and the bow is ours. Retrieve it.'

Without hesitation, Karl crawled into the open and began making his way across the ground towards the flight case. Lasers and machine-gun fire, with the occasional explosion from grenades, continued all around him.

As soon as Karl was away, De Flores too broke cover and dashed to the nearest dead Cyberman. Pulling the arrow from its chest, he ran back behind the wall where he had sheltered. He examined the arrow closely, although he had confirmed everything he suspected with a glance at its shining head.

On the rooftop, Richard's attention was caught by something. 'My lady. Who is that little man?'

Lady Peinforte fired another arrow, this time narrowly missing her intended target. She glanced across in the direction that Richard was indicating.

'Who knows?' she replied, reaching for another arrow. 'Some interfering . . .' she stopped, and peered more closely. Suspicion dawned. 'It cannot be,' she whispered.

'His face has changed,' said Richard.

'The wench's too. But . . . of course. Why, toads and adders can be leaders of men, can the Doctor not change his face?'

A slight gust of wind blew the smoke from the burning buildings, clearing the air for a moment. Near the crater, the TARDIS was suddenly visible. Lady Peinforte was exultant. 'O glorious evil,' she cried. '*It is he!*'

* * *

'Where did it come from?'

The object of Lady Peinforte's unconfined joy was crouched with Ace near the crater, examining the arrow that had killed the Cyberman. Now the Doctor was at last prepared to give his companion undivided attention, and his face was deadly serious.

'I couldn't see,' said Ace.

'Cybermen killed by a bow and arrow?' said the Doctor. 'It's ludicrous . . .' A thought struck him. 'Unless . . .' he said, half to himself. He pulled the arrow out of the chest panel. It glinted. 'Of course. The head's made of gold.'

Ace was impressed. 'That's real gold?'

'The only substance,' the Doctor replied, 'to which Cybermen are vulnerable.'

'Classy,' said Ace. She reached out to touch the arrow head. The Doctor snatched it away.

'Gold dipped in poison.' Ace froze. 'Lady Peinforte's signature.' He looked around them carefully. Fifty yards away, the last paramilitary apart from Karl and De Flores was fighting a losing battle with the remaining Cybermen who were steadily closing in on him. There was no sign of anyone else. Ace shivered.

'I really think we should get out of here, Doctor,' she said.

The Doctor agreed. 'I think you're right. Now,' he mused, 'the Cybermen and Lady Peinforte both hate me to the death. The others mustn't feel left out.'

He darted across the open space. The bow lay shining in the open flight case where De Flores had left it. The Doctor took the bow and snapped the case shut. He turned back to Ace.

'Come on,' he said. Ace needed no encouragement: together they bolted to the TARDIS.

On the rooftop, Lady Peinforte watched in horror as the Doctor took the bow. This development had played no part in her calculations of imminent victory. 'No,' she screamed. '*No!*' She hastily loaded her bow and took aim at the Doctor's fleeing back. But the door of the TARDIS was closing behind Ace before Lady Peinforte could fire; the deadly poison-tipped arrow slammed into the already-closed door. A second later the TARDIS had dematerialized and was gone.

Absorbed as Lady Peinforte and Richard were in these actions, neither of them noticed Karl snaking foward across the ground towards the flight case. Lasers flashed over his head but he continued, and retrieved it. He then leapt to his feet and ran full-tilt back across the scorched ground to where De Flores was waiting in the shelter of the partly finished house. Without a word being necessary, they dashed through the building to the back and were through the perimeter fence and into their waiting vehicle as the Cybermen lumbered into the front of the house. As the sound of the engine starting and moving off reached the Cybermen, the Cyber Leader raised a hand and the pursuit was abandoned. There were more important matters that demanded their attention.

The Cyber Leader turned to his Lieutenant. 'Bring the bow at once,' grated the metal voice.

There was the slightest hesitation before the Lieutenant replied: 'The Doctor and the female companion have escaped with it, Leader.'

'Escaped?'

A sudden rattle, similar to that of a Geiger counter, attracted their attention. They turned towards it. A Cyberman was passing a scanner over the body of the Cyberman from which De Flores had removed Lady Peinforte's arrow. The Cyberman responded immediately to his Leader's unasked question.

'Terminated by another human female using gold, Leader,' he said.

The Cyber Leader tightened his fist. 'The bow must be located at all costs.' His voice had risen slightly. It became even more ominous. 'We must also discover who this woman is.'

In the crater, two other Cybermen began to use their lasers to cut the statue from its rocket sled. The two separated almost instantly and more of the rock crust covering the statue fell away. As it did so a sudden great wind seemed to descend from above, as if pushing down on the earth.

Wakened by it, one of the policemen lying on the ground some distance away stirred groggily and opened his eyes. It seemed to him that he saw a number of tall, silver robotic figures, and approaching them two men, identical twins, wearing silver headphones. As he stared in disbelief, all the robots gathered near the crater where the comet had landed. They seemed to be holding a silver statue of a beautiful woman. All the time the rushing wind from above grew stronger and stronger. He could hear it now. Dust and stray paper blew all around him. He looked up, but could see nothing and yet the sense of some large physical object was so strong he shivered. Strangest of all, the robots, statue, and the men seemed to begin to disappear from the tops of their heads downwards. After a moment their heads had vanished, and for a bizarre instant they became headless robots. The descent of invisibility, however, continued relentlessly: shoulders, torsos and legs steadily disappeared in a matter of seconds until there was nothing to be seen at all except the rocket sled. It was only then that there was another sudden rush of wind, this time much shorter than before, and then calm normality returned to the atmosphere. The policeman reached with difficulty for his radio and pressed the call button. The radio did not respond.

In a field outside Windsor, the TARDIS materialized. Out stepped the Doctor, carrying the eerily glowing silver bow like a water-diviner's branch. Ace followed. It was almost as though the bow were pulling the Doctor along, with a momentum emanating from its own secret nature. 'Aha,' the Doctor called back over his shoulder, 'I was right.' He cackled happily. 'They're moving the statue.'

Ace looked disapprovingly at the bow. 'I really don't like this stuff,' she said.

'You shouldn't,' agreed the Doctor. 'Validium was created as the ultimate defence for my planet Galli-frey. Fortunately, it's never been used. None of it should ever have left, but as always with these

59

things . . .' His eyes hardened and his voice paused, momentarily interrupted by some distant memory, '. . . some did.'

Ace began to see the connection. 'So you had to stop Lady Peinforte . . .' she began.

'Or anyone else,' interrupted the Doctor.

'. . . ever putting the three bits together.'

'So,' nodded the Doctor, 'I launched the biggest one into space.'

'But you got the sums wrong.'

The Doctor sighed. 'Yes,' he admitted. He stared sadly into the distance as they continued to hurry along, the bow still pulsing with silver light. 'Instead of going into a permanent circle, every orbit was bringing it back to its point of departure. It was only a matter of time.' To Ace's relief, given the expression of such deep sadness on his face, the Doctor's attention was drawn back to the bow. 'Ah,' he said, 'we're getting close. Look.'

The bow had begun to buzz slightly, and the light flashing from it was now becoming slightly brighter.

'I'd feel a lot safer tracking them inside the TARDIS,' Ace complained

The Doctor, however, was firm. 'The Cybermen might trace the TARDIS. This way we let our validium find theirs,' he told her.

'Isn't that a bit old-fashioned?' asked Ace.

The Doctor looked at her and smiled. 'I'm an old-fashioned guy,' he said.

Another, admittedly different, old-fashioned guy, in the form of Richard, was at that moment peering nervously round the corner of a back street at the cars passing a few yards away. Lady Peinforte wrapped the glowing silver arrow back in its cloth and pointed firmly in the direction of Windsor High Street. Richard quailed.

'My lady,' he ventured, 'there are people there.'

Lady Peinforte snorted indignantly. 'Of course there are people. This is Windsor. Come.' She marched past him. Richard took a deep breath, crossed himself, and followed.

Oblivious to the stares and giggles they were attracting, Lady Peinforte strode along the High Street with something approaching pleasure.

As Richard and she passed, two skinheads leaning against a wall outside an off-licence nudged each other and began to follow.

As De Flores had ordered, Karl pulled the van to a halt in the lay-by. De Flores reached into his inside jacket pocket and pulled out a large leather wallet. He unfastened it and took out a number of gems and some currency. These were evidently not of immediate concern to him. Finally he located a small pouch and, pulling the string which fastened it, shook into his hand a quantity of gold dust.

He glanced up at Karl's interested expression, and carefully poured the dust back into the pouch.

'You are wondering what the gold dust is for, Karl,' he said, and smiled bleakly.

Karl nodded.

'Eventualities,' said De Flores. 'Drive on.'

* * *

In a clearing in the forest outside Windsor, the grass suddenly stirred as a strong wind rushed downwards at it. It flattened in a large circular patch. There was a powerful and hypnotic humming sound which grew steadily louder in volume, growing to a crescendo. The birds in nearby trees scattered. Having reached its height, the sound suddenly stopped.

On the edge of the clearing there was a ruined crypt: bleak, stark, and eerie.

Outside, the silence seemed to grow more intense. This time the Cyber spacecraft did not need to conceal itself; it flashed into visibility and hovered to a landing. The panel door slid open and the Cybermen began to emerge. They carried among them the statue of Nemesis.

'Are you looking at me?' said the smaller of the two skinheads, stepping firmly in front of Lady Peinforte. He and his larger friend had followed her and Richard through the town, and now, on a deserted road on the outskirts, they had made their move. Lady Peinforte, however, was firm.

'Stand aside,' she said imperiously.

The second, and larger, skinhead belched and took a swig from the can of lager with which he had been refreshing himself. He looked Richard up and down, obviously assessing his weight and height and apparently finding it deficient. Richard said nothing. 'What are you?' the bigger skinhead demanded suspiciously. 'Social workers?'

'Out of my lady's way,' said Richard.

The two skinheads sneered scornfully at his shoulder-length hair and then ignored him.

'We want to tell you our problems,' the smaller one leered at her.

Lady Peinforte recoiled in disgust from the stink of tobacco on his breath. 'Will you,' she asked ominously, 'be turned into rats?'

The two skinheads laughed, the smaller one taking advantage of his colleague's inattention to relieve him of the can of beer. 'We already have been,' the fat one was telling her ladyship. The two boys collapsed in a fit of laughter. Lady Peinforte and Richard remained stonily silent. The mirth faded at the skinheads' leisure, to be replaced by the expressions of threat of which it had been only another form.

'Poor rats,' said the smaller skinhead dangerously. 'That's our problem.'

He produced from inside his jacket a ninja fighting stick with which he attempted a series of impressive manoeuvres. These were clumsy but the weapon, as Richard immediately understood, was none the less formidable.

'Money,' said the second skinhead.

Lady Peinforte and Richard looked at each other. It was left to Richard to speak. He turned back to the two skinheads. 'Money, say you?' he asked politely.

The crypt contained a heavy stone sarcophagus covered in cobwebs, inside which lay the statue, glowing slightly in the semi-darkness. Above it, mounted on the wall was a carved stone sign which read 'Death Is But A Door'. Also looking down on it were the Cyber leader and his Lieutenant, who effortlessly pushed shut the stone lid of the tomb. Another Cyberman descended the steps leading from the ruined tower of the small building.

'The remaining validium approaches, Leader,' he reported in the usual monotone.

'Activate the communications unit,' replied the Cyber Leader calmly.

The Lieutenant reacted to this, interrupting as the Leader turned away. 'But the Doctor and Peinforte are still to be destroyed,' he said. His words stopped the Cyber Leader short. He turned back to face his second-in-command.

'Do you question my authority?' the Leader asked.

Even Cybermen prevaricate. He paused momentarily. 'We should wait before communicating,' he finally said.

'And will you answer for the delay?'

This was evidently too much to contemplate. The Lieutenant gave the required command at once. 'Activate!' he ordered sharply.

A Cyberman pressed switches on the portable communictions console set up in a corner of the crypt. Tiny red lights twinkled in the dusty darkness, reflecting dully on the ancient marble of the tomb to state that a transmission signal had been emitted. An amber light flashed briefly, informing the operator that it had been instantaneously received in the further reaches of distant space.

The Cyber Leader's voice boomed and echoed from the old stones inside the dark tower. 'Our victory is inevitable,' he pronounced. 'The Doctor cannot conceal himself, as he is carrying validium. And when Peinforte sees what is awaiting her here, the shock will cause her the immediate condition of insanity. Remember, this is why we chose this position. She is a simple savage accompanied by a terrified peasant.'

Several fields away the two skinheads were attempting to yell for help through the gags which bound their mouths tightly, although one could be forgiven for assuming their muted noises were screams of pain. They were certainly suffering enough for this to be believable, hanging as they were side by side and upside down from the branch of a tree. Both were now clad only in their underpants, their hands and feet tied. The smaller one was suspended by his feet from the branch by means of his ninja fighting stick. On the top of the fire burning immediately beneath them were the now charred remains of their clothes. The proximity of the flames meant that the skinheads had constantly to jerk about to reduce the areas of their bodies that were being scorched. These discomforts, however, paled into insignificance as far as either of them were concerned, given their audience. A few yards from their defenceless faces, although as yet keeping carefully away from the fire, four lions watched them motionlessly.

The skinheads' entire hopes of liberty and life for the future were at that moment centred on the two distant figures they could see approaching them through the forest. Unfortunately, their attempted yells through the gags had as yet failed to attract the attention they desperately needed. The two seemed entirely intent on the objects they were carrying. The girl's attention was obviously focused on the bizarre ghetto blaster to which she was evidently listening on headphones, while the strange man's was occupied by the thin metal object which he was carrying in a peculiar way, as though they were both following it. As they emerged from the trees it could be seen that this was a bow, flashing with strange silver light. Their voices drifted across.

'I'm sure I'm nearly getting something, Professor,' said Ace.

The Doctor was hurrying on. 'Static,' he said shortly.

'Listen,' Ace told him. She flicked a switch on the ghetto blaster. Sound came through the speakers: a distorted electronic burst. The Doctor, however, stopped, his ears pricking up as instantly as a dog's. His eyes narrowed.

'You could be right after all,' he agreed slowly.

'Could be, shmould be,' said Ace. 'It's definitely an alien device: it must be the Cybermen.'

The Doctor smiled indulgently. 'But,' he told her gently, 'they're scrambling their signal. If we try to make sense of that we could be here for ever. Much better to find them with our eyes and ears. Come on.'

But Ace remained where she stood. An idea had occurred to her. 'What,' she said, 'if we jam their transmission?'

'I suppose it might interfere with the coding . . .' The Doctor looked at her anew. There were quite frequently moments when she surprised even him.

This, he realized, was one. '. . . so we could listen in. Not bad. Have you got anything handy?'

Reaching into her pocket, Ace triumphantly pulled out a cassette. It was the one she had bought from the jazz band at the pub after their untimely summons into their present circumstances. Recalling the Doctor saying there was no time for her to obtain it, she said with a certain playfulness: 'This do?'

The Doctor grinned. 'Perfect,' he replied.

Ace slotted it in and pressed the play button. They waited intently, too absorbed to notice the strained but faint and gagged cries for help drifting towards them from the nearby tree.

'Commence final phase,' the Cyber Leader grated at the communications console operator. 'Repeat. Commence final phase.' Lights twinkled on the console and the transmission, coded instantly, was transmitted immediately. The Lieutenant shifted.

'I must repeat my objection to the transmission of incorrect data, Leader,' he said again. The Leader turned to him slowly. He continued undeterred, however. 'Our force does not,' he emphasized, 'yet possess all three units of validium.'

There was a silence. 'You are outside your function,' grated the Cyber Leader.

The communications console operator cut in. 'Your transmission has been received, leader.'

The Cyber Leader nodded slowly in satisfaction. 'Repeat once more,' he said, 'then relay the response.'

Suddenly, the entire communications console began

to emit a high pitched screech. Warning lights flashed erratically. The Cybermen moved around it.

'Report!' the Cyber Leader said to the console operator.

The operator hurriedly checked his readings. 'Interference,' he said quickly. 'Transmission and reception affected.'

'Interference?' the Leader was so ominously calm he might simply have been requesting a weather report. 'From what source? Provide more information.'

There was a delay as the computer checked and double-checked the circuits. The Cyber Lieutenant listened in to the interference impatiently. He was at a loss. 'It's a completely unknown form of sound, Leader,' he reported.

'Open the monitor facility,' ordered the Cyber Leader. The console communications operator did as he was told and flicked the switch.

The crypt was flooded with the honking and swooping wail of a saxophone-led jazz quartet. The computers simultaneously registered negative results to the demands for information regarding the identity of the sound. The Cybermen looked at each other, presumably in incomprehension.

The music swung out into the sky, into the ether, into space. It bounced, a tiniest fraction of a second later, off the moon, and travelled billions of miles from star to star, across the universe.

'Monstrous,' said Ace in delight as the cassette turned silently in her ghetto blaster. 'That should keep them busy.'

The Doctor chuckled in agreement. 'I love a jam session,' he said. 'Come on.' They hurried forward, Ace carrying the tape player. Suddenly they were stopped short by the astonishing sight which met their eyes. Two skinheads with very red faces and wearing only their underpants, were hanging upside down, bound and gagged, from the tree in front of them. Overcoming their surprise, the Doctor and Ace approached them. The Doctor produced his penknife and cut the gag from the mouth of the nearest one. 'Who on earth did this to you?' asked the Doctor in amazement.

'Social workers,' came the terrified reply.

Only a few hundred yards away, the social workers themselves were creeping slowly and with extreme care through the woods towards the crypt, when they came upon a gleaming silver structure. It looked to Richard the size of a palace. Although neither he nor Lady Peinforte had any way of identifying it as the Cyber spacecraft, their instincts connected it with the tall silver creatures without need for even so much as a glance passing between them. Thus they had begun to make their way slowly and silently through the trees and bushes which surrounded it before even seeing the two large identical men wearing silver ornaments on their heads – neither Lady Peinforte nor Richard possessed the information to be able to identify these as headphones – who were evidently guarding it.

They continued skirting through the undergrowth and were almost past the spacecraft when they were frozen by the nearby roar of a lion. It was a casual, rather than a belligerent, roar, but to two people who had never heard one before it was extremely disturbing. Richard immediately fell to his knees. Even Lady Peinforte was rattled. She kicked him and, as ever torn between his obeisances to God and herself, he took the line of least resistance and rose reluctantly to his feet, looking about him in terror.

'My lady . . .' he began in a whisper.

'Of course I heard it,' Lady Peinforte interrupted tersely. 'Am I deaf?'

'It sounds like a bear,' whimpered Richard. 'But worse.'

Lady Peinforte unwrapped the arrow and examined it. It was buzzing and now almost transluscent, pulsating with an ever brighter light.

'See,' she said urgently. 'We are near the Nemesis.' She wrapped the arrow in its cloth again, although even this could not now conceal the extraordinary quality of light radiating from it. 'Come,' she said with her usual firmness. Richard hesitated. Lady Peinforte raised an eyebrow threateningly. 'The bear will not pursue us. Such things happen only in the theatre.' She marched forward. As usual, Richard followed reluctantly. Emerging from the forest, they stopped, stunned.

Ahead of them, a small herd of giraffes grazed peacefully.

Richard found his voice. 'What creatures are these?' he asked in horror.

This time Lady Peinforte was noticeably shaken. 'I know not,' she admitted.

'They will eat us.' Richard gave way at last to complete panic. He fell to his knees, this time in front of Lady Peinforte. 'I beg you my lady, return us to our own time. England now is full of terrors.'

Lady Peinforte immediately regained control of herself at the suggestion. 'You are mad,' she replied coldly. 'Return without the Nemesis? Never. And without my knowledge,' she added, seeing the desperate look in his eyes, 'you cannot return at all. I tell thee Richard, either you'll assist me and we gain it or I will leave you here for ever. Now come. I think they are peaceful.'

Richard stared about himself wildly. 'What place,' he asked, 'what place is this?'

Lady Peinforte turned to him with a peculiar intense relish. 'This piece of ground on which you stand? Why I will tell you. It is thy grave, Richard.'

Richard was petrified with shock and disbelief. His entire body felt cold all over. He could manage only a terrified whisper.

'What?'

'Yes,' said Lady Peinforte sweetly, enjoying her moment. 'I ordered that you should be buried here when I planned my tomb. See,' she pointed to a small and withered piece of rock planted in the ground at their feet, 'there was your stone. If the dogs would not eat thee, I ordered you put out here, to attend me in the next world as in this.' She made a large sweeping gesture with the arrow and pointed grandly out of the trees. For the first time, Richard saw the dark tower on the edge of the clearing. 'Because here, you see, is mine.' Lady Peinforte was possessed with an excitement Richard had never seen in her before. His senses reeled. Lady Peinforte's voice continued inexorably. 'And aptly, the silver creatures there do hold the Nemesis. We shall attack.'

She loaded her bow with a gold-tipped arrow, motioning to Richard to do the same. In a dream, he did so. Lady Peinforte strode forward. Too terrified to remain alone on the awful spot where he stood, Richard reluctantly followed her once again. Leaving the cover of the woods they passed a sign which neither of them could read. Printed on it in large white letters was the message: 'Stay in your car while in the safari park.'

In the bushes, the Doctor and Ace lay still and watched them pass. 'Good,' said the Doctor quietly. 'Very good.'

Quietly and with extreme care, Lady Peinforte and Richard approached the tower, their bows at the ready. There was no movement from within. They reached the doorway; all was silent. They burst inside.

The crypt was deserted.

The arrow, however, was shining so brightly that it illuminated the inside of the tower with the power of several arc lights.

Richard lowered his bow in relief. 'There is nothing here,' he said unnecessarily.

'See the arrow,' hissed Lady Peinforte. 'The statue is here, depend on it. Quietly, Richard.'

They began to search, Richard warily avoiding the

tomb. Lady Peinforte noticed, and sneered. 'Rather fine, is it not?' she said proudly. Immediately she was possessed by a sudden fit of rage. 'But where is the statue of Nemesis?' she screamed. 'Where is it? Where?'

Her voice carried without difficulty to the nearby thicket in the forest where the Cybermen were hiding. The Lieutenant turned to his Leader as the cries reached them. 'Is this the human condition of madness, Leader?' he asked.

'It is,' came the reply. 'Kill them.'

The Cybermen moved stealthily forward into the open towards the tower. As they did so, Lady Peinforte's screeches continued to travel towards them.

In the tower the arrow was flashing uncontrollably. Lady Peinforte was beside herself with fury and frustration. 'It must be here,' she was yelling. 'It must be.' Judiciously keeping a watch at the door, Richard saw the Cybermen leaving the cover of the forest and making their way towards them.

'My lady,' he said urgently, reaching for an arrow and loading his bow.

Lady Peinforte, however, was unhearing, running her fingers up and down the walls. 'It is here,' she muttered. 'It is. The arrow tells me.'

Taking careful aim at the Cyberman in the centre of the group, Richard fired.

The arrow embedded itself in the ground. Automatically the nearest Cyberman reached out and tested its composition. The others paused momentarily and turned.

'Gold,' reported the Cyberman. They immediately

turned back towards the forest. As they did so, Richard fired again. This time the arrow lodged in a Cyberman's chest panel. He turned to inform Lady Peinforte that he had almost no arrows remaining, but he could see at a glance she was incapable of hearing. She had been seized with inspiration. 'Of course,' she breathed, transfigured. 'Help me, Richard. Help me. It's in my tomb.'

Richard was appalled. Lady Peinforte, however, would stand for no argument. 'Help me,' she repeated menacingly. With extreme distaste, and shuddering with terror, Richard began helping her to remove the ancient stone lid.

6

The Doctor and Ace had crept away from the vicinity of the crypt and were peering cautiously through the undergrowth at the Cyber spaceship. The two men with silver headphones were still guarding it. The Doctor had been wrestling with a mental problem, though he now seemed to have solved it. He turned to Ace decisively. 'I don't suppose you've completely disobeyed my instructions and secretly prepared any nitro-nine have you?' he asked with a seemingly casual air.

Ace knew him too well to be deceived. 'What if I had?' she countered defensively.

'You naturally wouldn't do anything so insanely dangerous as to carry it round with you, would you?'

'Of course not, Professor. I'm a good girl and do what I'm told.'

'Excellent,' concluded the Doctor with satisfaction. 'Blow up that vehicle.'

The Cybermen were suffering badly from Lady Peinforte's gold-tipped arrows fired by Richard, despite responding with their laser beams. The Cyberman with an arrow lodged in his chest panel was beginning to die, writhing on the ground, and there was an almost desperate note in the Cyber Leader's voice as his commands barked through the trees. 'Destroy them. Destroy them,' he ordered.

The Lieutenant moved nearer to him and spoke. 'We cannot sustain these losses, Leader,' he said. 'We must withdraw.'

The Cyber Leader turned on him quickly. 'No,' he said. He was emphatic. 'We must hold the statue and take the arrow from them.'

An arrow hissed through the air and embedded itself in a tree a few feet away from them.

'If we are overcome,' the Lieutenant argued, 'our entire strategy will fail. The Cyber race will cease to exist.'

There was a deathly silence. The Leader's circuits checked and double-checked the rationale of the Lieutenant's statement. Finally he was forced to speak. 'Your logic is correct,' he replied heavily. 'Their supply of gold is limited.' He turned to the remaining Cybermen, who were firing laser beams at the crypt, and called: 'Retreat.'

They began making their way back through the forest towards the spaceship.

The two men were still standing on guard, large, silent and immovable, one at either end of the craft when to their surprise the Doctor suddenly appeared from the bushes in front of them and politely raised his hat. 'Good afternoon,' he called. 'I'm the Doctor. You wanted to kill me.'

Before they could recover themselves he was gone,

bolting into the forest. The guards looked at each other, drew their guns, and ran after him.

No sooner had they disappeared into the trees than Ace appeared, darted to the spaceship and threw a can of nitro-nine under it. She ran quickly back into the forest and dived behind a large tree.

As she did so, the out-of-breath guards came into sight of the returning Cybermen: of the Doctor there was no sign. The Cybermen stopped in surprise. The two men stopped too, realizing the Doctor had gone to ground somewhere nearby. Before they could alert the Cybermen, however, there was a loud explosion from behind them. Their jaws dropped and they turned to see what was left of the Cyber spaceship engulfed in flames.

To the Cyber Leader only one explanation was possible. His reaction was instant. 'Betrayal,' he said matter-of-factly. 'Kill them.'

Before they could explain or even protest, the guards fell to the laser fire of the Cybermen.

Ace, making her way quietly to where she could see the Doctor was hiding, stopped in horror. The Doctor, however, waved to her and together they ran off. Glimpsing a movement, the Cyber Leader spotted them in the distance, against the background of the smoking ruins of his spaceship. As the Doctor flitted away, recognition dawned upon the Cyber Leader.

In the crypt, Lady Peinforte and Richard had at last succeeded in removing the heavy stone slab that for three hundred and fifty years had served as the lid of her ladyship's tomb.

The brilliant silver figure of the statue of Nemesis lay inside. Lady Peinforte was ecstatic. Richard, however, had other concerns. 'But my lady,' he asked, 'where are your bones?'

Lady Peinforte picked up the arrow and held it out to the statue, staring down into the sarcophagus with an expression of childlike wonder. The statue gave an intense sudden glow of silver light which shone from the entire surface of its body.

'What matter?' Lady Peinforte replied tersely. The arrow, in her hand was flashing like a beacon, dazzling them with its bright silver light. As if in response, the statue began pulsating simultaneously.

Arriving back outside the TARDIS, the Doctor and Ace stopped for breath. The Cybermen were a safe distance behind and, for the moment, were not an immediate threat.

Noticing that Ace was unusually subdued, the Doctor looked quizzically at her. There was a pause.

'They killed them,' Ace eventually said. Her voice was shocked. 'Just because I blew up the ship.'

'They'd already killed them,' said the Doctor firmly.

Ace looked at him in surprise.

'Cybermen create other Cybermen out of human beings by first enslaving their minds,' the Doctor continued. 'The ones on guard there were only partly processed. Mentally, they were destroyed a long time ago.'

The full horror of the Cybermen's evil struck Ace for the first time.

'You mean that's why the Cybermen saved my life?' she asked. 'So they could do that to me?'

The Doctor nodded sadly. 'They used to be like human beings themselves,' he said. 'Quite a few people have tried to follow their example.' He dismissed the Cybermen from his mind. 'Enough of them,' he said briskly, and turned his attention to Ace's ghetto blaster. Looking up again a moment later, however, he could see she had still not managed to forget the frightful scene she had witnessed. Ace looked up at him, saw the thought in his eyes and nodded in confirmation.

'I still don't like it,' she said.

'Nothing about the Cybermen is likeable,' replied the Doctor. 'Are we still jamming their transmission?'

Ace looked. 'The tape's still running,' she responded.

'Good,' said the Doctor. 'Now let's find out who's listening to it.'

He turned up the volume. Jazz blew once again across the English woodland.

'Mmm,' murmured the Doctor appreciatively. 'Sweet.' He switched on the machine's holographic projector.

Two of the kind of people the Doctor had described as trying to follow the example of the Cybermen were at that moment only a few hundred yards away. De Flores and Karl stood waiting as the Cybermen approached them. The Cybermen stopped. De Flores held up a hand in greeting. 'We want to talk to you,' he said. The Cybermen waited. De Flores, apparently unabashed, continued. 'I don't know if you're familiar with Wagner's *The Ring*,' he said, with all the social ease of a man conducting an interval chat at a Vienna Opera House. The Cybermen, as ever, looked blank. De Flores explained. 'We,' he said, 'are supermen. But you . . . you are giants. Wonderful creatures.'

'Of course,' returned the Cyber Leader. 'But why should we form an alliance with you?'

De Flores became animated. 'We had a leader once,' he said. His eyes gazed far off. He was suddenly looking back fifty years. 'He predicted your coming. Now, together, we shall fulfil his vision and enslave the world.'

'Together?' The Cyber Leader would have laughed in contempt had he been capable of laughter. 'Cybermen need no help from any race.'

'But,' Karl interrupted, 'a woman who is almost less than human now holds the statue.' The Cybermen looked at Karl for the first time.

'While we have the bow of Nemesis,' continued De Flores smoothly. 'She now holds the arrow and the statue itself, yet she is armed,' he permitted himself a complacent chuckle, 'with only primitive toys.'

'You insult us?' the Cyber Leader asked, without a trace of expression.

'Of course not,' replied De Flores hastily. 'But whatever your . . .' he searched for the most diplomatic phrase, 'unfortunate vulnerability, it does not affect us. We can remove her for you.'

Karl gestured slightly with their two machine-guns. It was not lost on the Cybermen. The Leader replied without hesitation.

80

'We accept,' he told them. 'Destroy the woman and her servant and we will divide the planet into your slave groups and ours. But remember, any betrayal will be fatal. We are invulnerable to your weapons.'

'Not so the woman and her servant,' replied De Flores smugly. He snapped his fingers at Karl, who handed him the machine-gun. De Flores weighed it appraisingly in his hands for an instant, then snapped back the safety catch. 'Ah,' he said with nostalgia. 'I feel young again. Come.'

He led Karl off at a sprightly pace into the trees, towards the tower. As soon as they were out of earshot, the Cyber Leader turned to the waiting Cybermen. 'As soon as they have the statue and the arrow,' he intoned, 'destroy them.'

With the monitor speaker switched off, the tape played on silently. Above the ghetto blaster the hologram remained blank, looking like a small globe of mist immediately on top of the machine. The Doctor drummed his fingers. 'Nothing there?' he asked in frustration.

'See for yourself,' replied Ace.

The Doctor glared at the hologram. 'That handful back there weren't the only Cybermen in the universe,' he insisted. 'We've only got to find out where the others are.'

Ace sighed. 'Look,' she said. 'This is the computer's reading of where their transmission signal is being received. Right?'

'Quite,' replied the Doctor.

'But according to the scanner,' continued Ace patiently, 'nothing is there.'

The Doctor gave a howl of rage. 'Then the scanner's wrong,' he yelled. He calmed himself with difficulty and spoke in a restrained manner. 'The ones we've seen are only the advance party. Out there somewhere,' he waved his arm across the sky, 'is the entire Cyber force and they want the Nemesis more than anything else in space.'

Ace looked at him doubtfully. The Doctor did occasionally make mistakes after all. 'How can you be so sure?' she asked.

'Because,' said the Doctor with great self control, 'validium is more incalculably destructive than I could possibly convey to you. It generates evil. It had to . . .' He stopped himself. Suddenly he looked at Ace anew. 'And because it's 1988,' he finished. There was a pause. Ace sensed there was more that he wanted to say and that it was difficult for him. The Doctor took a deep breath and continued. 'When I launched the Nemesis, the orbit I gave it brought it back past the Earth every twenty-five years. Look back over your own century. It first appeared in 1913.'

'The eve of the First World War,' said Ace in wonder.

'Twenty-five years on . . .' the Doctor prompted her.

'1938.'

'Hitler annexes Austria.'

Ace was beginning to see the pattern. '1963 . . .' she began, but the Doctor completed it for her.

'Kennedy is assassinated.'

Ace looked at him with real fear. She hardly dared ask, but knew that she had to do so. '1988?' she said quietly.

'Check the scanner again,' said the Doctor.

Out of the corner of his eye, Richard sneaked a glance at Lady Peinforte. She had still not stopped gazing at the statue of Nemesis; she seemed to be communing with it in some silent, mysterious way that he could not begin to understand. The arrow and the statue now glowed as one with an almost blinding intensity.

'How perfect you are,' breathed Lady Peinforte ecstatically to the statue. 'Oh, how perfect. Immaculate beauty carved in absolute evil.'

Richard could not bear it any longer. He had to tell her what was on his mind. 'But where lie your bones my lady?' he asked desperately. Lady Peinforte did not give any indication of having heard. 'They must be buried,' he added emphatically.

With an enormous effort, Lady Peinforte appeared to wrench her attention away from the statue. 'What matter?' she hissed. 'They are dead. But I live. And soon I'll have the bow ...' she shuddered with pleasure, 'and my Nemesis will be complete.'

Richard was shocked at the change that had come over her. It was as though the statue's presence had induced in her a trance-like state.

A sudden burst of machine-gun fire from outside ripped through the window. Bullets tore across the wall above them. Lady Peinforte and Richard ducked. 'We are attacked,' shouted Lady Peinforte unnecessarily. 'Quickly. The arrows.'

83

Richard was seized by fear. 'We have but one left,' he told her. 'And I do not think our arrows can stop these weapons.' He stole a cautious look out of the window which told him everything he needed to know: De Flores and Karl with their submachine-guns were advancing briskly towards the tower.

Lady Peinforte, however, had other ideas. 'Nonsense,' she told him briskly. 'Make it count. They destroyed the silver creatures.'

As though in mockery, a second burst of fire tore through the doorway, shattering bits of plaster off the sarcophagus. Richard panicked. He turned to his mistress. Suddenly he felt very calm. 'See, lady,' he said. 'We have no chance.'

Lady Peinforte stared in disbelief. 'No. They cannot take the Nemesis,' she said, 'not now I have it.' She put her arms round the statue, cradling it like a child. 'They cannot.'

Richard looked back through the doorway. De Flores and Karl were only yards away. He fired the last arrow. It shot through the doorway. De Flores and Karl threw themselves to the ground as the arrow flashed over their heads. They remained still, evidently fearing another. Lady Peinforte was groping inside her tomb. There was a creak, and a section of the wall of the crypt suddenly swung back in a shower of cobwebs, revealing itself as a hidden door. Richard was open-mouthed in surprise. Lady Peinforte smiled grimly. 'Not for nothing did I design my own tomb,' she said, and pointed at the ancient inscription on the wall. 'Death is but a door. I always knew I'd cheat it. Help me with the statue.'

Outside, Karl and De Flores were raising themselves cautiously on to their elbows. Richard implored her. 'We cannot lift it, lady. We must fly.'

Ignoring him, Lady Peinforte began pulling at the statue hopelessly.

'Put up your hands,' said a voice. They turned to find Karl standing in the doorway, with De Flores behind him. The machine-gun was aimed directly at them.

Even so, Lady Peinforte was defiant. 'Never,' she said unequivocally, standing in front of the tomb.

Richard's reaction was different. He immediately fell to his knees. 'You want the statue, masters?' he cried. 'Here, take it. Take it.'

Lady Peinforte looked down at him in the utmost contempt. 'Thou feeble . . .' she began.

'And here is the arrow,' continued Richard, snatching it away from her and holding it out to them. 'See?' He threw the arrow into the tomb.

There was a devastating flash of light which seemed to burn through the stones of the tower to the core of time and matter itself. Even though he had closed his eyes in preparation at the last second, Richard was stunned. Karl and De Flores, however, were not expecting it and were unable to move or, temporarily, to see. 'Forgive me, lady,' shouted Richard and, grabbing her by the waist, he threw her over his shoulder.

Lady Peinforte screamed from the depths of her being. 'Unhand me. Nooo!' Ignoring her protests, Richard forced her through the newly opened doorway into the entrance to the secret passage. Karl, recovering, found the trigger of his gun and fired a burst of bullets into the blazing light, but the door had already swung closed behind them. Karl ran to it and began feeling the wall, trying to find a way in. De Flores recovered himself, and approached the Nemesis in wonder, fluttering a hand at Karl in passing. 'No matter Karl, no matter. They are of no importance.' His voice was shaking with wonder. 'We have the statue, the arrow . . . and the bow. We can destroy all creation.' He looked at Karl triumphantly. 'Wagner unfortunately must be rewritten. The supermen must control the giants.'

'But how are we to control the Cybermen?' asked Karl.

'Gold overcomes them,' said De Flores. 'We have no such weakness.'

There was a sound of movement inside the sarcophagus. They turned and looked into it. The statue's right hand had grasped the arrow and was closing slowly on it.

'See,' said De Flores, 'how the statue prepares for life. The arms adjust their position to receive the weapons.'

Karl stared at the Nemesis, mesmerised. De Flores, although unable to transfer his gaze from the statue, none the less clicked the silver flight case unlocked and opened its lid carefully. 'Our first task then,' he continued, 'will be to take control of the extra-terrestrials.'

There was a slight sound at the doorway behind them. The Cyber Leader, flanked by two Cybermen, had arrived. There was the slightest pause before he spoke. 'Unfortunately,' he said, 'that will not be possible.'

De Flores backed away, nearer to the statue. A note of panic entered his voice. 'Keep away,' he shouted. 'I possess the entire statue of Nemesis. All power is mine. The life and death of everything in existence is in my hands.'

The Cyber Leader sounded almost patient. 'Then where,' he asked, is the bow?'

For the first time De Flores, aghast, looked down at the flight case. As he did so, his face turned ashen: the case was empty.

On the grass outside the TARDIS, the being who could have supplied the Cyber Leader with his answer had he been so inclined, namely the Doctor, gazed at the bow, deep in thought.

Next to him, Ace once again scrutinized the holographic image of the Earth and Moon above her ghetto blaster. The cassette turned silently in the body of the machine, but thousands of miles out in space, the jazz quartet's music bounced off the moon and continued into the infinity of the universe. In front of Ace, the tiny red lights of the graphic equalizer twinkled, but otherwise there was no activity and nothing else to be seen in the image but endless empty space.

Suddenly the Doctor gave a shriek. All the birds for yards around fluttered rapidly into the sky.

'Of course,' he yelled. 'It's so simple.' He leapt to his feet in excitement. 'Keep your eyes on the hologram.'

Ace, who had been doing nothing else for almost two hours, found this more than a little unnecessary. 'There's nothing there,' she replied shortly.

The Doctor jumped up and down. 'They are there!' he insisted. 'But they're shrouded.'

Without waiting to explain, he began punching buttons on the front of the tape player. The music suddenly became audible through the speakers.

'You what?' asked Ace.

'Shrouded,' he repeated. 'They don't show up. But,' he continued hitting switches, 'if we keep jamming their communications they'll be forced to reveal themselves.' He completed his adjustments to the controls. The music increased in volume. The Doctor checked his arrangement of the switches. 'Bass . . . treble . . . O please let me be right.' He suddenly appeared to catch himself out. 'Who am I talking to?' he asked aloud in surprise. 'Balance.'

The music reached a crescendo. As it did so, tiny dots began to appear on the hologram in the vicinity of the moon. They multiplied and spread like a rash across the screen.

The Doctor recoiled in shock. Ace was petrified.

'What . . . what are they?' she managed to ask.

'Focus,' said the Doctor. He further adjusted the tape deck's switches. The holographic image zoomed in and selected three of the tiny dots around the Moon. As Ace watched, they became larger, sharpening into visibility. A giant spacecraft with two smaller ones in attendance hung ominously in space over the Moon. At last the Doctor answered.

'Cyber warships,' he said quietly. He tore his gaze

from the image and turned to face her. 'Thousands of them. And they're invisible.'

Ace paled. Her mind was reeling at the shock of the image in front of her. The Doctor was clearly very deeply disturbed. 'And it's all my fault,' he whispered. He switched off the hologram sharply and they sat in silence, stunned with shock. Ace noticed distantly that a light drizzle had begun to fall, but it seemed as if it were happening somewhere else, a long way off.

At length she roused herself, forcing herself to speak. 'What,' she began hesitantly, 'what can we do?'

The Doctor looked up at her, as though surprised to remember she was present, so deeply did he appear to be immersed in the terrible problem that confronted him. His eyes were distant and strange. Suddenly he became his normal jaunty self and he smiled cheerfully. 'I think our best move,' he said brightly, 'is to walk into the crypt with the bow.' He sat back and looked at Ace with satisfaction.

Ace stared at him blankly. 'Professor,' she asked, 'are you losing your marbles?'

The Doctor leaned forward. 'We've got to get the bow into the statue's hands to activate the validium,' he told her firmly.

'But there is just one little problem isn't there?' Ace reminded him. There were moments when she really had to take care of the Doctor. 'We won't just be able to walk straight out again, will we?'

The Doctor, however, seemed unsurprised at this. 'No,' he agreed briskly, 'we certainly won't. We'll have to keep the Cybermen talking for some time.'

'And this is the only way,' asked Ace doubtfully.

The Doctor smiled reassuringly. 'I've always believed in the direct approach,' he said. Then he became serious. He put his hand on her shoulder. 'You can still make it back to the TARDIS,' he said quietly.

Ace flared. 'Are we going or what?' she said, already on her feet.

Side by side, they walked out of the trees and into the open. The bow in the Doctor's hands was pulsating with silver light. Ahead of them, the dark tower of the crypt stood dark in the grey rain, silent and suffused with an eerie sense of danger.

Inside the crypt, at least as far as De Flores was concerned, all was far from well. 'Surely we can negotiate this . . .' words temporarily failed him, '. . . misunderstanding,' he desperately concluded, facing the expressionless Cybermen. The empty bow case yawned at him, seemingly in cavernous mockery.

The Cyber leader was imperturbable. 'Our understanding is perfect,' he replied. 'You thought you had all three components of the statue and naturally wished to destroy us.'

'You're completely mistaken . . .' Karl attempted, putting his best learned lessons to frantic use.

The Cyber Leader lifted his weapon fractionally. 'Silence,' he said unnecessarily.

Suddenly the statue moved. The tomb shook and the quality of light emanating from it changed just enough to divert their attention to itself momentarily.

Even the Cybermen turned. As they did so, De Flores slipped a hand into his pocket.

The Cyber Lieutenant turned to his Leader. 'Validium activity indicates the proximity of the bow, Leader,' he said.

'Excellent,' the Cyber Leader replied calmly. 'Kill them.'

As the Cybermen turned to obey the order, De Flores's hand came out of his pocket, casting a golden cloud over them. The thought flashed into Karl's brain that De Flores' eventuality had indeed arisen. There was no time, however, to reflect on his mentor's foresight. The Cybermen looked like human beings caught in a swarm of hostile wasps. The gold dust affected them all instantly and they doubled up, turning and trying to escape it. The air of the small stone room was filled with the rattling of their alarm. De Flores and Karl took immediate advantage of the confusion. Pushing past the struggling Cybermen, they charged outside. The Cyber Leader was the first to rally himself. 'Pursue them,' he croaked. The Cybermen followed De Flores and Karl into the outside air.

The fleeing pair were nearing the cover, if not assured safety of the edge of the forest when Karl leaped onto De Flores, bringing him to the ground. They rolled, struggling on the grass as the Cybermen caught up and surrounded them.

'You fool,' panted De Flores at his protégé. 'They're going to kill us.'

Karl got to his feet and looked down at the elderly

man with contempt. 'Herr De Flores,' he said, 'your day is over.'

De Flores stared wildly at him, and looked hopelessly round at the Cybermen. 'You betray me?' he asked in astonishment. His voice became almost plaintive. 'Have I taught you nothing?'

'Everything,' replied Karl, apparently with complete satisfaction, 'which is why we now part company.' He smiled, and gestured to the Cybermen. 'I'm afraid,' he told De Flores, 'you fail to understand history in addition to Wagner.'

De Flores looked as though he could not believe his ears. 'I?' he stuttered.

'Supermen are all very well,' Karl continued smoothly. Suddenly his tone became steely. 'But the giants are the master race.' He turned to the Cyber Leader triumphantly. 'Here he is,' he said, indicating the crumpled figure at his feet. 'Now make me one of you.'

There was a pause as the Cyber Leader seemed to consider the proposal. Finally he came to a decision. 'You show potential,' he replied. 'Very well.' He turned to his Lieutenant. 'Have them both programmed at once,' he ordered.

De Flores and Karl were led away. The Leader addressed the remaining Cybermen. 'We must complete the statue immediately,' he said firmly. 'Locate the bow. Destroy the Doctor and his companion.'

7

In a thickly overgrown part of the forest a quarter of a mile away, the bushes rustled, indicating the approach of human beings to the wildlife in the area. As the birds flew hurriedly away the undergrowth parted to reveal Lady Peinforte, now led by Richard.

Behind them the dark mouth of a passageway yawned in the shadows.

Richard blinked in the daylight and breathed deeply in inexpressible relief. He had not expected to ever see the sunlight again. He turned to her ladyship. She looked pale, dazed and disoriented. He led her to a rock and helped her sit down on it. She allowed him to do so as though she were in a dream or drugged. Richard looked at her in concern. She stared in front of her, apparently unseeing, entirely occupied with her inner world.

Richard coughed and, when this failed to elicit any reaction, spoke gently. 'How is't with you my lady?' he asked.

There was a pause. He was not sure whether she had registered his question, and was about to try another when at last, wearily, she replied.

'I understand not,' she said distantly. She was still not facing him.

'What's to understand?' asked Richard.

There was a long silence. Lady Peinforte appeared to be wrestling with a major problem. Finally she took a deep breath and looked at him directly for the first time. 'Always I have treated you badly,' she said slowly. 'I have done you no service, shown you no kindness. Yet,' she hesitated, 'yet you risk your life to save me. Why so?'

'Should I not?' asked Richard.

Lady Peinforte laughed bitterly. It was her customary laugh, harsh and cutting. Yet there was a softness in it too which he had never heard before. 'I do not live in the world of should,' she said emphatically. 'But you . . . you are a good man, Richard, and I am evil.' Richard looked at her, filled with profound sadness. He was also relieved, knowing now the moment had arrived.

'My lady,' he said softly, 'we have no more weapons.'

Lady Peinforte's moment of vulnerability snapped closed like a book. Her expression was replaced at once by its usual cold demeanour. 'You are wrong,' she replied with her familiar icy firmness. 'I have one more yet that will not fail: my knowledge. I will have the statue of Nemesis.' She rose to her feet.

Making their way towards the crypt the Doctor suddenly became aware that Ace was no longer beside him. He stopped, and looked round.

She was standing still a few paces behind him, an

expression of indecision on her face. 'Doctor . . .' she said, and halted. She evidently did not know how to say what was troubling her. The Doctor looked at her in his kindliest manner and smiled encouragingly.

'Ace?' he said.

'Look,' said Ace. 'Let's be honest, right?'

'By all means. Are we ever anything else?'

'I've never bottled out of anything before, but . . . I'm really, really scared, Doctor.'

The Doctor put his hands on her shoulders. 'I'm sorry Ace,' he said. 'Forgive me.' There was a pause. 'Why don't you go back to the TARDIS?' he added carefully. 'You'll be safe in there whatever happens.'

Ace's doubts were immediately resolved. 'No chance,' she said instantly.

The Doctor opened his mouth to continue but she anticipated him and cut off his speech before he had uttered a syllable. 'I said no chance, Doctor.' Ace's jaw was set firmly in the manner that the Doctor knew meant there was no arguing with her. 'I'm coming with you,' she said, and, picking up the tape player once again, hurried forward towards the dark tower.

The Doctor sighed, and beamed after her in admiration as he moved to follow. He knew all along he had been right about Ace.

Unfortunately, neither of them noticed that the tape, which was still playing silently, was about to reach its end.

Inside the crypt, Karl was also smiling in satisfaction as the final attachment for Cyber programming was

95

fitted to De Flores' body. The Cyberman responsible stepped back and pressed the preliminary switch.

A few feet away, at the communications console, things were not proceeding so happily. 'The Cyber Fleet is still not receiving our transmissions, Leader,' said the Lieutenant.

The Cyber Leader was perplexed. He reviewed the situation again, and once more reached no conclusion. 'Is there any pattern to the jamming signal?' he asked, exasperated.

'It is meaningless,' replied the Lieutenant tonelessly.

'Let me examine it,' ordered the Leader.

The Lieutenant pressed a switch and the monitor speaker opened up. The crypt was flooded instantly with the music of the jazz quartet. The Cybermen stood still, bemused.

The music came to its finale and ended. The sound of cheers and applause which replaced it stirred a deep, long forgotten and almost extinct wisp of memory in the Leader's brain cells. He scanned them to attempt to identify it.

'I have heard that sound before,' he said slowly.

The applause continued, mixing with cheers, whistles, and cries for more. The the sound stopped and there was a loud click. The communications console instantly sprang back into life: lights reilluminated, circuits were once again complete, and the normal buzz of healthy electronic activity became audible once again.

The Lieutenant turned immediately to the Leader.

'Transmission channels are clear again, Leader,' he reported perfunctorily.

'Splendid. Their arrival is imminent.'

Weakly, De Flores struggled in his technological prison. 'You fool,' he croaked. 'The statue's power is nothing without the bow.' He rattled his wires desperately but to no avail, and fell back against the wall. His eyes were turning purple and his face was deathly white. The Cyber Leader glanced at him contemptuously, but could not resist speaking for the benefit of his Lieutenant.

'We shall shortly obtain the bow,' he replied.

De Flores cackled with the laughter of the deranged. He was clearly exerting all his considerable mental power to countering the programming energies, although clearly growing weaker by the moment. 'Obtain it?' he repeated. 'From the Doctor?' he cackled again. 'You delude yourself. He is no common adversary.' De Flores summoned the last of his waning strength to draw himself up to his full height. 'Do you imagine,' he boomed imperiously, 'he will simply walk in here and hand it over?'

'Good afternoon,' came a familiar voice. In astonishment, they all turned towards the doorway where Ace and the Doctor stood, the latter raising his hat politely with one hand. In the other he held the bow of Nemesis.

There was a cataclysmic silence. Even the Cyber Leader was overcome, although he was the first to speak. 'Doctor,' he managed.

The Doctor smiled cheerfully. 'Yes, here we are,' he confirmed as though they had arrived a few minutes late for a tea party after a minor parking problem. 'Sorry we couldn't be here earlier, but we were held up on the way.' His voice echoed in the stunned silence. The Doctor was fully in charge of the moment, and enjoying himself tremendously. He gestured courteously to Ace. 'You remember my companion Ace, of course?' he looked around at them all anxiously for confirmation.

As he did so, the Cyber Leader uttered a metallic snarl and snatched at the bow. The Doctor, however, was far too quick for him and skipped nimbly aside.

The Cyber Leader glared at him. The strength of the Cyber Leader's will was so palpable that Ace shuddered. Although she was still in the doorway, Ace noticed that in dodging the Cyber Leader, the Doctor had deliberately moved well inside the crypt. She could see no escape for him now.

The Cyber Leader broke the silence. 'What do you want?' he asked thickly.

The Doctor grinned at him and gave the bow an affectionate stroke. This was not lost on all the crypt's occupants, whose eyes moved as one in fascination to it. When they looked up again for his reply, the Doctor was smiling indulgently at them.

'You Cybermen do go in for obvious questions don't you?' he said, with mock sadness. 'But then you always have talked in such a dull way. You know, everything's always . . .' and he adopted an extremely convincing Cyber voice, 'Kill him, or Excellent.' The Cybermen started in reaction to the insult but the Doctor was back to his own voice again and still ahead of them. 'So what do I want? Well, obvious questions beg obvious answers. Nothing. That's what I want.' He looked at the Leader with apparent concern. 'Have I lost you?' He spoke clearly, as though to a child. 'No-thing. Nothing.' And suddenly he became steely. 'Nothing lasts for ever.'

The Cyber Leader made a dismissive gesture, as if to cut through the swathes of unnecessary talk he was enduring. 'Give me the bow,' he rasped.

But the Doctor moved out of reach again, and again, Ace noticed, further into the crypt and among his deadly enemies. 'Patience, patience,' he admonished. 'I thought we'd have a little chat first. Relive old times. Look to the future.'

'You have no future,' replied the Leader, with flat finality. 'Neither does your companion, nor any of her race.'

As the metallic voice grated, Ace was stealing a glance at the Nemesis. It was brighter than she had ever seen it, and its intensity was increasing by the moment, as though the entire statue were preparing for massive and unimaginable activity. It was reacting to the bow, which she now saw was shining equally brightly in the Doctor's hand. Ace began to see the Doctor's purpose. The Doctor, meanwhile, was replying to the Cyber Leader, and holding the attention of all the other beings in the crypt.

The Doctor seemed blithely unconcerned at the imminent destruction of himself, Ace, and the entire planet on which they stood. 'I'm afraid I have to disagree with you,' he was saying cheerfully. The Cyber Leader, however, had clearly suffered as much delay as he was prepared to tolerate. He held up an imperious silver hand.

'Enough,' boomed the voice, 'we shall complete the statue.'

The Doctor ignored him. 'There is, however you care to approach it, always a future,' he ruminated.

Ace took a deep breath. Despite the Doctor's seemingly boundless confidence, she felt things were bad enough without his going off on one of his lengthy discourses on the subject of time. It was, after all, his favourite theme, with which like a jazz musician with a good tune, he never ceased finding new aspects to explore and develop. Unfortunately, the present wasn't the perfect moment for his thoughts on the future. The Cyber Leader evidently agreed. 'Take the bow from him,' he ordered harshly.

'And for some of us,' continued the Doctor as though he had not heard, 'it arrives too soon.'

'Look!' shouted Ace. She was unable to stop herself. The most extraordinary light she had ever seen was radiating out of the tomb. As they turned to look, cracks appeared all over the tomb. Smoke began billowing out of it and it disintegrated. As it did so, the statue rose to its feet, bursting into blazing light. All the humans present involuntarily stepped back; even the Cybermen seemed nonplussed.

The whole crypt was flooded with radiant light. All the remaining rock that had been covering the statue fell away and it stood entirely revealed for the first time. The reality of it took Ace's breath away. She was looking at a living silver image of Lady Peinforte.

Amid it all, the Doctor stood happily, looking about

himself and rubbing his hands in apparent satisfaction. He winked at Ace and smiled. 'That seems to be in order,' he said, and nodded at the door.

Ace needed no further hint. As one, they bolted through the entrance and were running hard across the grass outside. To her surprise, Ace noticed the Doctor was still holding the bow.

'TARDIS,' he puffed. 'The statue will follow this.' He held up the bow as he spoke and, still running, they disappeared among the trees.

8

At the far edge of the forest, near the road, Richard started in surprise at a distant rumbling. At first he took it for one of the cars he had seen in Windsor, but his countryman's hearing soon differentiated between them and the deeper, more sinister sound he now heard. The ground began to shake beneath him. Lady Peinforte, however, was unmoved. 'Fear not, Richard,' she said. 'It is the Nemesis come alive.'

Richard stared at her, chilled to the marrow of his bones. 'Alive?' he gasped.

'Why, yes,' replied Lady Peinforte calmly, as though it were the most natural activity possible. 'Which means it is complete.' Her face hardened and set. 'And now it shall be mine.' She gazed into the distance. 'Why, I shall be mistress of all that is. All that shall be. All . . .' her voice rose to a screeching crescendo, 'all that ever was. Yes, all. *All* . . .'

Richard understood in that moment that Lady Peinforte had gone completely mad. He was filled with pity for her. He put his hand on her arm. 'Come, lady,' he said gently, 'let's find some shelter.'

Lady Peinforte turned on him furiously. 'How dare you?' she screamed, staring at his hand on her arm as though he were as leper, begging for coins. Richard immediately withdrew it, and as quickly his expression of warmth and care was replaced by the servant's professional mask.

'I shall lead and you follow,' screamed Lady Peinforte. Her madness seemed to seize her completely. Her voice rose to an unearthly shriek. 'There is no alternative!' With this she marched off through a thicket of gorse. Richard painfully followed.

They emerged by the side of a road. Occasional cars passed. Fifty yards away, a young man stood by the roadside with his thumb out. Richard reached the road in time to see a car pull up in response to this signal, and the young man clamber in. The car moved away.

Ahead of him, Lady Peinforte was speaking over her shoulder. 'We needs must walk, Richard. We have no craft.'

Richard caught up with her. 'We can avail ourselves of one of these steeds, my lady,' he said. 'I know the method of it. Sit you here and rest awhile.'

To his surprise, she concurred without a murmur and sat down on a milestone. Richard put out his thumb at a passing car, and was surprised when it passed without stopping. Her ladyship, however, did not notice.

'All that is, and shall be . . .' she murmured.

Lavinia P. Hackensack, widow, of New Haven, Connecticut, called to the chauffeur of her Lincoln Continental to pull over. Something about the pair of hitch-hikers engaged her attention. Thus the door opened as Lady Peinforte rose to her feet and approached the car; her ladyship was inside the vehicle before Mrs Hackensack had even finished asking her where she and her young man were headed.

Inside the now ruined crypt, there were only two figures left. Karl was freeing De Flores from the Cybermen's programming console. Their laughter echoed round the rafters of the tower.

'Herr De Flores,' Karl repeated, wiping the tears from his eyes, 'your day is over.'

'You betray me?' gurgled De Flores. 'Have I taught you nothing?' He shook off the last of the wires and stretched. Then he patted Karl on the back and together they made for the door.

Inside the limousine, the cocktail bar, television, and the ankle-deep carpet proved of no interest to Richard or Lady Peinforte, preoccupied as they both were with the experience of rocketing along at thirty miles an hour.

'You folks students?' ventured Mrs Hackensack happily.

Lady Peinforte ignored her. Richard hastily tried to attract Mrs Hackensack's attention to himself. 'Alas,' he spread his arms expansively, 'I am but a servant, madam, and cannot read or write. My lady is of noble birth and has some Latin and a little Greek.'

Mrs Hackensack smiled. 'I guess you're on vacation right now?'

Lady Peinforte continued to stare out of the window, intent on the passing scenery.

Richard desperately tried to think of something else

to say with which to occupy Mrs Hackensack. 'Go you far, madam?' he asked.

'Me? Oh, I just came over from London.'

Richard nodded. 'Two days' ride,' he said sympathetically.

Mrs Hackensack looked surprised. 'No, the traffic was pretty reasonable. I left about forty minutes ago.'

'Forty minutes?' Richard was astonished.

Mrs Hackensack nodded, agreeing the journey could have been quicker. 'Well, I'm in no hurry,' she said. She was warming to this young man with his courtly manners. 'As a matter of fact,' she told him, 'I'm here on vacation, checking out my roots.'

At last, here was a term Richard understood. He nodded eagerly. ''Tis wise with crops this time of year.'

Mrs Hackensack did not notice. 'My family came from around here,' she continued. 'I traced them way back to the sixteen hundreds.'

Dimly aware at last that there was someone else in the conveyance, Lady Peinforte decided to inform her of the imminent change in the nature of the universe. She leaned towards Mrs Hackensack confidentially. 'All things,' she informed her, 'will soon be mine.'

Richard nearly fainted. Fortunately, Mrs Hackensack seemed undeterred by the news. She patted Lady Peinforte on the hand. 'I guess they will, honey,' she agreed. 'Education's the key to the door. Always has been.'

Lady Peinforte gazed at her earnestly. 'Time past,' she said with great seriousness, 'present and future; power invincible; the secret of the heavens.'

Mrs Hackensack nodded, seeming to understand. 'Connecticut's heaven, if you ask me,' she said. 'My family owns a little land there, just a couple of hundred square miles. They used to own land in these parts too. The Hackensacks of Hackensack Grange?'

Lady Peinforte suddenly bridled, appearing to pay attention to her for the first time. 'I know them,' she snapped. 'Thieves and swindlers all.'

Mrs Hackensack was thrilled. 'You study history?' she asked.

'Dorothea Hackensack,' said Lady Peinforte with great intensity, 'did bribe away my cook.'

Mrs Hackensack's expression clouded. 'You lost me,' she said. 'Let me see, there was a Dorothea. Died around sixteen . . .'

'. . . twenty-one,' interrupted Lady Peinforte with relish. ''Twas a slow poison.'

Richard realized he did not know how to open the doors of the car. Escape was impossible. He closed his eyes.

Mrs Hackensack was open-mouthed. 'This is unbelievable . . .' she murmured.

'Many found it so,' agreed Lady Peinforte.

'Here I am driving along and I pick up someone who's researched my family tree.'

Lady Peinforte smiled at her. 'We ride to destiny,' she said.

Mrs Hackensack smiled again. 'We sure do, honey,' she agreed. 'We sure do.'

The building site looked just as ordinary to Ace as it had the first time she saw it. Which, considering the fate of the universe was about to be decided on it, she thought was perhaps after all only as it should be. The Doctor had no time for such reflections. He hurried out of the TARDIS, rubbing his hands, and looked about himself appreciatively. 'What fun we had here last time,' he remarked. 'Right. The statue should arrive any minute. Now everything depends on my final calculations.'

Ace looked at him anxiously. 'It's OK,' she said. 'I promise not to interrupt you.'

A shadow crossed the Doctor's face. 'There is a slight problem,' he admitted, 'in that we're likely to be attacked by the Cybermen at any minute. I can't allow myself to get the figures wrong this time.'

For a moment he looked like a small child. Ace grinned reassuringly. 'Don't worry, Doctor,' she said, and patted him on the hand. 'I'll look after you.' She pulled out her catapult.

'Ah,' said the Doctor with enthusiasm. Rummaging through his pockets he produced a small pouch, which he opened and spilled the contents into her hand. A number of gold coins glinted in the watery sunlight. 'Aim at the chest panel,' he said. They each caught the other's eyes. Suddenly they were looking at each other with the utmost seriousness. Ace realized the Doctor was depending on her as he had never had to do before. She nodded slightly to let him know she understood. The Doctor smiled. 'I trust,' he said portentously, 'you remember my strict instructions that you're never to cause any future explosions?'

Ace put on her best little girl's face. 'I'm a better person as a result, Doctor,' she replied politely.

'Good.' The Doctor grinned confidently. 'We'll be ready for anything.'

Ace squeezed his hand and was gone.

The Doctor watched her run across the wasteland and disappear into a large empty warehouse. For a moment, a flicker of worry crossed his face, but he dismissed it with difficulty and searched again among his pockets to discover his abacus. He turned his concentration on it and began moving the beads at a ferocious rate.

At times during the next quarter of an hour or so, Ace could be glimpsed at various points around the building site. At one moment she was visible through the glassless upper window of a half-completed house; at another she was to be seen digging in the mud near the site's entrance, then again flitting into the large and as yet undemolished warehouse that had evidently formed part of the original site. Inside the building, the vast space had clearly been in disuse for many years as the weeds growing everywhere attested.

The Doctor continued to be exclusively absorbed in his calculations. Since they were both so preoccupied with their tasks, it was not for some minutes that they became aware of a distant strange, unearthly sound that was growing nearer. Ace was the first to hear it. Initially, it seemed to suggest a kind of wailing wind, as though all the disharmonies ever heard in the world had combined simultaneously to provide an awesome cacophony. As it grew nearer, this seemed to become a deep, ominous rumble, like continuous growling thunder.

The bow of Nemesis, lying on the ground at the

Doctor's feet, began to react, buzzing and pulsating with intense silver light. Dimly aware of it, the Doctor, however, did not allow his mind to stray from his calculations, and the abacus continued to click as rapidly as before.

The daylight darkened almost completely. In the course of less than a minute there was the effect of an almost total eclipse. The only source of light in the area now was the silver bow, which shone like a laser beacon into the gloom as the Doctor struggled with his work. He was so absorbed that he did not even look up. But then he had no need to do so; he knew perfectly well that the massive changes in sound and light meant the statue of Nemesis had arrived.

When he finally did look up in a second's respite from the massive mathematical problems which possessed him, the statue stood complete, holding the bow. The light from inside the Nemesis abated steadily to a bright silver radiance. The light was of a different quality now: cold and sharp, calmer and yet somehow more deadly than before. The sound the Nemesis had brought with it had faded entirely to be replaced by an eerie quiet. Slowly, almost cautiously, the daylight returned.

The Doctor noticed Ace standing near him staring at the Nemesis. The statue's metal eyes looked ahead, seeing yet unseeing. Ace shivered. There was for her a great sense that she stood in the presence of something unimaginably destructive.

Still rushing mentally headlong through a vortex of figures, the Doctor pointed silently to the rocket sled as the abacus continued to click under his fingers. As

Ace watched, the Nemesis moved and climbed slowly on to the sled. The Doctor nodded absently and took no further notice of either of them, reabsorbed in his thoughts.

Ace suddenly realized as she stared at the Nemesis that it was now looking down at her from the rocket sled. She froze. Then the statue opened its mouth.

'I am beautiful, am I not?' the statue asked. The voice was cold, clear, and deathly calm.

'Yes,' said Ace. She looked back at the statue. 'You're very beautiful.'

The corners of the statue's mouth twitched slightly in the merest imitation of a bitter smile, perhaps more of a grimace. 'It is only my present form,' said the voice. 'I have had others which would horrify you.' There was the slightest pause. 'I shall have both again.' The words hung in the air. Ace gazed on in fascination. 'You are surprised I speak?' asked the Nemesis.

Ace struggled to find her voice. 'I . . . I know you're living metal,' she replied.

Again, the statue seemed almost to smile. 'I am whatever I am made to be,' it said calmly. 'This time Lady Peinforte named me Nemesis, so I am retribution.'

Ace became aware that a sudden wind had picked up. Debris blew past her feet and she shivered again. The stare which the statue had directed at her was so intense that she looked away, towards the entrance to the building site. At the gateway she saw a group of Cybermen. There appeared to be seven of them, including the Lieutenant and the Cyber Leader.

'Catch you later,' she said to the statue, and ran towards the buildings. The statue did not respond.

As soon as Ace was gone, the clicking of the abacus stopped, and the Doctor at last looked up. His eyes met those of the statue and for an instant an understanding of some kind seemed to pass between them.

9

Ace peered cautiously over the window-sill of what would eventually become a front bedroom of the half-completed house if, she reflected, the house ever got completed; if there was ever a world left for it to be completed in. Below her, the Cybermen were carefully advancing, spread out and silent, their laser weapons at the ready.

Ace took a deep breath and let it out slowly to calm herself. Whatever happened, they must be kept away from the Doctor until he had finished and could set the rocket sled on to its correct course.

At that moment she was jolted back to reality by a loud explosion. A cloud of smoke enveloped the Cybermen, and for an instant she could glimpse them floundering uncertainly, looking about them for the source of the attack. Ace grinned to herself.

She took out the first of the gold coins and loaded it into the sling of the catapult, then, remembering the Doctor's firm injunction, took careful aim at the chest panel of the nearest Cyberman. She drew the catapult elastic taut; there was a second's pause, then she fired.

The Cyberman's reaction was even more immediate than she had expected. The coin evidently lodged inextricably in his chest panel and the ugly death-rattle began instantly. The Cyberman keeled over, clutching desperately at his chest as the others turned to observe him, it seemed to Ace, in slow motion. For a few seconds she watched, fascinated, and then as their heads began to turn in search of the position of the attacker, she remembered herself in time and was running from the room and down the stairs.

The Cyber Leader, however, his reactions a milli-second quicker than those of his inferiors, had glimpsed her as she turned from the window. His voice grated thickly: 'Destroy the human female.'

The other Cybermen scanned the area, their lasers ready. The Cyber Leader's voice reached a semitone higher. 'Find and destroy her,' he said.

The Cybermen spread out around the half-completed building and began to search for Ace. They peered through the empty windows into the uncompleted rooms but there was no sign of her on the ground floor. At a signal from the Lieutenant, three of them moved purposefully inside.

Once in the house, they double-checked the downstairs rooms. The interior of the understairs cupboard was blasted with lasers but contained no human female. The unfitted kitchen was empty, as was the unfinished living room. The house shook as the heavy steps of the Cybermen clumped up the stairs, but even this failed to frighten their target into making a break for freedom. Upstairs, the bathroom and bedrooms too were empty.

Outside, Ace carefully completed her silent descent of the drainpipe and reached the ground. For the

flicker of an instant a memory crossed her consciousness of slipping equally silently down the drainpipe at
the back of a semi-detached house in Perivale, as her
parents sipped their bedtime drinks. The thought
registered just long enough for her to catch herself
wishing she were safely back there, before she was
moving again, creeping carefully to the corner of the
building. Having checked there was no Cyberman
guarding the doorless front entrance, she crept forward and entered the house.

In the hallway, she pulled the catapult from her
pocket and tugged a second gold coin from the pouch.
She loaded the sling.

As she did so, the heavy tread of the Cybermen
thudded on the ceiling above her head. They were
moving from the bedroom towards the stairs, evidently having decided to continue their search.

Ace slipped quickly out of the front doorway and
stood to one side of it, listening intently, with her back
against the wall. The heavy steps moved along the
upper passageway to the top of the stairs. The boards
creaked and the tone of the next step was different:
the first Cyberman had stepped on to the top of the
staircase. It took another step; then another.

Ace swung into the doorway, tightening the catapult elastic as she did so. Her small figure framed in
the light gave her a moment before the descending
Cyberman spotted her. This was just long enough to
give her a bearing on his chest panel as she brought
the child's weapon up to her own eye level. Automatically, his weapon raised.

Ace fired first, in the instant of surprise. The coin

sparkled through the air as the deadly laser sought to find her, and was immediately followed by the pure ring of a metallic note, clear as a tuning fork, as it lodged itself in the Cyberman's grating. Ace did not stay to see the results of her action but she had no need to do so. As she fled across the open space of the building site she could clearly hear the heavy crashing as the creature tumbled helplessly down the stairs. Ace gained the cover of another incomplete house and hid in a front room. Cautiously, she peered over the window ledge but she had evaded any pursuit. The other two Cybermen emerged at the bottom of the stairs and stood for a moment looking down at their stricken companion. Two down, five to go she thought; not bad for a beginner. She wondered how the Doctor was managing with his sums.

No sooner had the question raised itself, however, than the Cybermen looked up and saw her. The lasers raised and fired instantly. This time they were much nearer the mark and the brickwork and unvarnished window frame next to Ace's face shattered into smouldering matchwood. Ace instinctively threw herself on to the floorboards.

For the first time, the deadly pursuit became entirely real. Behind and across the room from her, a large smouldering hole had suddenly appeared in the wall. Ace caught her breath, and carefully pushed back the feeling of shock and terror that threatened to grip her uncontrollably. The only possible course was to keep the Cybermen's attention entirely concentrated on herself and away from the Doctor, whatever the cost.

Keeping this thought clearly in the forefront of her mind she stood up, next to the ruined window frame, in time to glimpse two Cybermen carefully making their way across the muddy open space, pitted with tyre tracks, towards the house were she was hiding. Ace rallied herself. 'Try to keep up,' she shouted, as contemptuously as a child. 'I've heard of metal fatigue, but you lot are pathetic.' With that, she rushed from the room and through the hallway towards the unfitted kitchen at the back of the house. The Cyber Leader's voice echoed after her.

'Kill her,' he shouted. 'Kill her.'

Ace ran into the kitchen, grabbing the door handle, and stopped. The door was locked. This possibility had not occurred to her. At the same instant she heard the steps of a Cyberman approaching round the side of the house. In a few seconds it would round the corner and she would be in full, and almost unprotected, view. Her only hope was to go back through the house. She turned and ran back into the hallway, only to stop as a laser blast demolished the bottom of the staircase next to her. The two Cybermen from the house opposite were very near indeed.

Ace was trapped. She heard the kitchen door behind her splintering as the Cyberman at the back of the house entered. Jumping on to the ruins of the staircase, she made her way upstairs as the Cybermen entered the building. She reached the top of the stairs as the first one came through the front door. Another laser blast blew a hole through the wall to her right as she swung out of sight on the landing.

Ace squatted down, facing the top of the stairs. From below came crashing and more splintering sounds as the nearest Cyberman stepped into the ruins of the bottom of the staircase, but this was followed by a solid step, as menacing as a single drumbeat, as his weight was taken by the first step which had not been damaged in the onslaught.

There was another step, followed by another, and another. The heavy, sinister, and purposeful footsteps of the Cyberman were followed by more. There were evidently two Cybermen now climbing the short staircase towards her. Ace's heart was pounding deafeningly, it seemed to her. She brushed at what felt like a cobweb on the side of her forehead and was surprised to see blood on her hand. She felt again and realized the brickwork blown off the wall as she reached her present position had shattered over the side of her face.

The footsteps were now almost at the top of the stairs, and the leading Cyberman about to step into view. Ace pulled back the elastic on the catapult and a third gold coin glinted in the unlit gloom of the landing.

The Cyberman saw Ace at the moment she saw him, but Ace had already fired. The gold coin once again stuck neatly into the chest panel and the now familiar rattle of death sounded immediately. The Cyberman she had struck fell backwards, tumbling down the stairs and taking down the one behind him.

Quietly, she began picking her way through the rooms towards the rear of the house. It was essential that the Cybermen were not able to track her movements by being able to hear her. Fortunately, the new

117

floorboards beneath her shoes were stiff and well laid, and she crept into the main bedroom without any reaction from below. Distantly, she could hear the Cyberman at the foot of the stairs disentangling himself from the one she had destroyed.

Reaching the window, she carefully looked outside and saw to her satisfaction that there was, as she had expected, a drainpipe nearby. She reached through the glassless window-frame and took hold of the pipe. She was just about to pull herself through prior to using the drainpipe to lower herself to the ground when a laser blast struck several feet below her, shattering the metal in her hand and scorching her arm. Ace drew in her breath in a gulp, silencing the cry of pain. She pulled back instinctively, catching as she did so a glimpse of a silver figure beneath her. A Cyberman was guarding the back of the house. 'Getting the idea, are we?' she whispered to it grimly. As if in reply, a second blast from below roared through the empty window and took out most of the ceiling above her head. There was an immediate rain of plaster, and the room suddenly acquired the appearance of being filled with dense fog. Given the glassless window, Ace knew it could remain so for only a few seconds, but that might be long enough to give her the time she needed. Loading the catapult, she crept through the opaque white dust to the window.

To the Cyberman below, she must have appeared like the apparition of death itself, she thought. Her face and hands appeared out of the white cloud suddenly, so that even before he had focused his weapon on her, the gold coin was lodged in his chest panel and the deadly rattle was sounding. For an instant the image of the statue of Nemesis crossed her mind . . . but at that moment she became aware of tramping steps coming up the stairs. 'Now what?' she wondered.

The footsteps reached the top of the stairs. Two Cybermen could be heard entering each of the upper rooms in succession, preceded by laser blasts. They were not taking any chances. When the bedroom door was blasted open and two simultaneous laser bursts tore into the room the dust had already cleared from the air.

There was no sign, however, of Ace: she was hanging by her fingertips from the window-ledge. With great difficulty, and as silently as was possible in the circumstances, she clambered back into the room. She could hear the heavy footsteps making their way down the wooden stairs. Quietly, she followed.

Outside, the air seemed pervaded with a strange scent which she was unable to identify. It was a faint but perceptible odour, sharp and cold. After a moment she realized it somehow emanated from the statue. Her head hurt where the shattered brickwork had hit it, and she felt nauseous and not a little light-headed. She wanted more than anything to lie down and sleep. The odour was so disturbing that for a second she again caught herself longing to be back in safe, boring Perivale.

This feeling lasted for only a second. There were, if her reckoning was correct, two more Cybermen to finish off. Even the Doctor would have to admit she had done rather well. She reached into her pocket and pulled out the pouch. To her dismay she discovered she had only one gold coin. Focusing with difficulty, she loaded it into the sling of her catapult.

She forced herself to move forward, and began making her way across the mud and puddles between the buildings towards where she had left the Doctor with the Nemesis. Perhaps he had finished by now. She had trouble walking in a straight line but insisted to herself that she did so. She approached another half-completed house and looked forward to leaning for a second on the wall at its corner as she passed. She reached it gratefully and put out her hand, touching the brick. It was at that point she heard the faint sound behind her. She was spinning round when the grating voice reached her.

'Still,' it rasped. Ace froze. Oh well, she decided, she had stopped most of them.

The Cyber Leader moved round the corner and stood in front of her, his laser weapon at the ready.

'Why?' said Ace. 'You're going to kill me anyway. Isn't that right?' She turned, disobediently, and as she had expected, the Cyber Lieutenant was poised behind her.

The Cyber Leader pushed her against the wall and both Cybermen moved in front of her, looking her up and down. 'We detect only one more piece of gold,' he said finally with something like satisfaction in his voice.

'Correct,' said Ace. Suddenly she raised the catapult menacingly. 'So,' she said, summoning the last of her strength. 'Who'll be next and who'll be lucky?' She aimed the coin directly at the Cyber Leader.

There was a pause. She swung fast to her left and aimed it at the Lieutenant, and then back at the Leader.

The Cybermen were nonplussed. The Lieuteneant spoke first. 'You have only one projectile left,' he said.

'That's right,' Ace agreed. 'But one of you has had it. Now which one's it going to be?'

In the silence that followed, Ace was sure the Cybermen could hear the pounding of her heart. Certainly it sounded to her as though a giant bass drum were being beaten invisibly between the three of them. Nothing moved. Finally, the Cyber Leader spoke. 'Kill her,' he said.

Ace glanced quickly from one to the other. Was this a trick? It must be. Then she caught the glint of light as the Leader's finger tightened on his trigger. She released the elastic and the coin lodged in his chest panel as she twisted her body aside. The laser blasted a hole in the wall immediately behind where she had stood, but the Cyber Leader was down, writhing on the ground. Ace bolted round the corner and was gone.

10

The Doctor was almost beside himself with the exhaustion of the mental efforts he had made during the course of the previous hour. The abacus whirred and clicked as his fingers flew over it. These sounds reached a peak, then suddenly, and almost miraculously, stopped. There was silence. The Doctor took a deep breath and let it out slowly. The statue watched him, silent and unblinking, its cold aura chilling everything around it.

The Doctor looked up. His eyes were bright. 'Got it!' he said to no one in particular. 'Now,' he began suiting the action to the word, 'we set the rockets to the correct time projection.' The small fins on the base of the rocket sled were carefully adjusted by his bony fingers. 'And you'll be . . .' he stepped back, 'right on course.'

For a moment he stood lost in thought, admiring his handiwork. Then a more serious idea seemed to strike him and he turned purposefully to the statue. 'Forward,' he said authoritatively.

The Silver Nemesis stepped delicately forward. It almost seemed to materialize in position. It took its former position on the rocket sled and waited, motionless, for the Doctor's next command.

The Doctor's voice remained firm. 'The rockets,' he announced to the Nemesis, 'are now locked on to your destination.' He smiled. 'Let's see how they're progressing.'

He reached for the ghetto blaster and switched on the hologram. The small vision of space appeared in perfect three-dimensional miniature in front of him above the weird machine. The Cyber fleet were ominously present, the tiny silver specks filling space around the Earth and Moon like a swarm. The Doctor appeared satisfied. 'Right on course,' he said, rubbing his hands.

A chill silver voice cut through the eerie silence. 'And I am to destroy the entire Cyber fleet,' said the Nemesis calmly.

'Forever,' replied the Doctor.

'And then?' asked the beautiful, deadly voice.

'Reform,' he said shortly.

The statue seemed to pause slightly, as though this answer were unexpected. 'You will need me in the future then?' it asked.

The Doctor's eyes were far distant. 'I hope not,' he said quietly.

The Nemesis gazed at him. 'That is what you said before.'

'That's enough,' snapped the Doctor.

The statue seemed cowed, but still it replied. 'And after this,' it said carefully, 'I will have my freedom?'

'Not yet.'

'When?'

'I've told you when,' said the most mysterious being in space and time. 'Things are still imperfect.'

The statue was silent. In the distance the Doctor caught sight of Ace unrolling a length of wire from the last buried cylinder of her nitro-nine. Steadily backing away from the explosive, she eventually attached the end of the wire to a hand-sized detonator and took up a position watching the corner around which she had recently escaped.

To the Doctor's horror, although there was no sign of the Cybermen in front of Ace, the Cyber Lieutenant and another Cyberman suddenly appeared behind her.

A slight sound from them seemed to alert Ace and she spun round fast. She was too late. The Cyber Lieutenant hit her with the back of his fist, knocking her sprawling. As she struggled to rise, the Lieutenant picked up the detonator and crushed it to a metallic pulp. Ace lay on the ground looking up at them. The Cybermen slowly levelled their lasers at her.

'Stop!' shouted the Doctor at the top of his voice.

Apparently surprised, the Cybermen turned and looked towards him, seeing him for the first time. This was not easy. He was crouched behind the rocket sled with only the top of his head visible to them.

'Harm her in the slightest,' he shouted, 'and I'll destroy the bow.'

The Cybermen lowered their lasers, and the Doctor stood up. The Cybermen looked at one another, then the Lieutenant nodded. The other Cyberman prodded Ace with his foot and she rose. The Doctor smiled encouragingly and moved casually round to the front of the sled as she crossed the no-man's-land between them without incident, arriving at the Doctor's side with relief. The Cybermen placed themselves at the rear of the sled and addressed the Doctor over it. Above them the statue of Nemesis remained motionless and aloof, as if hearing and seeing nothing.

The Cyber Lieutenant spoke calmly. 'Give us the bow, Doctor,' he said.

There was a pause.

'No,' replied the Doctor firmly.

'Then we shall simply take it and kill you both,' replied the Lieutenant. His statement sounded almost reasonable.

'Ah,' replied the Doctor. He appeared to be considering an invitation to tea.

'In any case,' continued the Cyber Lieutenant softly, 'your threat was meaningless.'

The Doctor looked up quizzically. 'Meaningless?' he repeated haughtily. 'How so?'

'How could you have destroyed the bow?' asked the Cyber Lieutenant.

'Well actually . . .' the Doctor began to explain. Not another lecture, thought Ace.

There was no stopping him. 'What I'd have done,' the Doctor went on, 'would have been to arrange for the bow to be neatly positioned behind the rocket sled. Then, and this is most important, I'd have arranged for the rockets to test fire at, say, a pre-arranged time.'

Automatically, following the line of his explanation, the two Cybermen obediently turned their heads, looking at the rocket sled behind which they were neatly positioned.

'By the way,' said the Doctor casually. 'What is the time, Ace?'

Ace consulted her watch.

'Almost . . .' she began.

There was a booming explosion. A massive ball of flame erupted from the rocket sled as the rockets test-fired. The Cybermen were engulfed and incinerated; when the flames faded a few seconds later only a few cinders remained on the ground where they had stood.

Ace was open-mouthed. The Doctor grinned. 'You're running a little slow,' he said kindly, and patted her on the shoulder.

The black smoke around them began to clear. Ace wiped her eyes, reopened them, and then froze. The Doctor, too, was very still. De Flores and Karl stood in front of them with their submachine-guns levelled. De Flores was smiling with quiet satisfaction.

'Oh, great,' said Ace.

De Flores ignored her, reacting as though it were the Doctor who had spoken. 'Yes, Doctor,' he said agreeably. 'We have all succeeded in deceiving the Cybermen.'

He raised his arm. Through the torn sleeve a metallic elbow glinted. Karl's shirt too was open at the top, revealing what had been his chest: it was partly metallized. 'A small price to pay, I think you will agree, for the successful fulfilment of our super-human dream.'

'The Cybermen made the mistake of assuming all human beings to be weak and corruptible,' added Karl superciliously. 'We, however, are loyal to the death.'

126

The Doctor was silent. He appeared perplexed.

De Flores calmly approached the statue and gazed upon it in apparent rapture. 'Now at last your long journey is over,' he said to it. 'You will be worshipped for ever.' The statue did not respond. De Flores waited, but no reply or even glance was returned to him. For the first time he seemed ill at ease. 'Doesn't she speak?' he turned angrily to the Doctor. 'Doesn't she speak?' he barked again.

'Not to the likes of you,' replied the Doctor.

De Flores' lips twisted in a thin smile. 'She will,' he replied. He regained his composure. 'Now Doctor, we must part,' he continued briskly. 'We thank you for removing the Cybermen. And now that you have kindly done so, the Nemesis is, at long last . . .'

'Yours,' said the Doctor. But he was looking behind De Flores. There was a sudden movement and Karl and De Flores spun round. The Cyber Leader was standing immediately behind them, his laser at the ready. There was a flash of light from it and Karl and De Flores were disintegrated before their fingers could tighten on their triggers.

'Sorry, Doctor,' said Ace, shocked. 'I thought I got rid of him.'

The Doctor was staring at the Cyber Leader. His eyes were steely. 'Don't threaten her,' he rasped.

The Cyber Leader almost shrugged. 'Give me control of the statue,' he answered.

'I can't'

'Then,' said the Cyber Leader with calm precision, 'I will kill her.'

The Doctor looked at the Leader as though the

Cyberman were a mentally deficient child. 'Didn't you hear me?' he shouted. 'I can't. Even if I wanted to.' He stepped right up to the Cyber Leader and stared at him closely. 'This is technology beyond your comprehension,' he added. 'It can't be reprogrammed.'

'To destroy the Cyber race?' said the Leader. 'No, Doctor. You will remove the rockets so the Nemesis cannot be launched.'

'That won't solve anything,' the Doctor answered. 'When the fleet arrives, the statue will destroy it just the same.'

'And the Earth with it,' concluded the Leader. 'The choice is yours, Doctor.'

'That's hardly rational.' The Doctor smiled icily.

The Cyber Leader suddenly seemed on the verge of entirely losing control of himself. He shuddered for a moment perceptibly. '*I shall destroy you now*!' he shouted.

'What's this?' asked the Doctor with extravagant courtesy. 'Hatred? Cybermen with emotions? Dear me, you're becoming defective.'

Ace closed her eyes. It was apparent the Doctor had gone too far this time. They were unarmed after all and ... Her thoughts were interrupted by a screeching woman's voice approaching from round the corner. Every head turned as Lady Peinforte, attended by Richard, appeared across the building site marching unnoticing through the puddles and mud. With a shock, Ace realized instinctively that Lady Peinforte was mad. 'All things,' she was shrieking. 'All power.' She laughed happily. 'Time,' she

128

informed a cement mixer in passing. 'Space.' She clambered over a pile of wood and continued across the site in a dead straight line towards the statue of Nemesis. 'The world!' she shouted, throwing back her head and laughing. She was soaking wet but did not appear to notice. In fact she was apparently unaware of anything at all except the statue which drew her like a beacon. 'The . . .' she was about to continue when at last she seemed to notice the group standing by the rocket sleds. 'Heavens,' she said, and gazed regally round, from the Doctor, to Ace and to the Cyber Leader, before finally resting her eyes on the statue, where her attention remained. She began to croon softly.

'She is mad,' said the Cyber Leader. For a second, the Doctor, Ace and the Cyberman were in agreement, but Richard interrupted before this could establish itself.

'Speak not of my lady so,' he said hotly, and glared at the assembled beings, unafraid and challenging.

Lady Peinforte, however, was beyond offence. She approached the statue slowly and in wonder. 'See?' she murmured to it, comfortingly, like a mother to a disturbed child, 'I am here.' She smiled reassuringly at it and continued humming softly.

'What,' asked the Doctor crisply, 'do you want?'

To everyone's surprise, Lady Peinforte heard, understood, and responded at once. She turned to him with a sudden air of normality. 'Why, my Nemesis, what else?' she replied.

'You're too late,' said Ace. 'The Doctor's got it.'

Lady Peinforte smiled with apparent serenity and

looked pityingly at Ace. 'It is incomplete,' she informed her, 'until it holds the bow. That can be given to anyone.' Suddenly, Lady Peinforte turned on the Doctor, and for that instant Ace felt the full chilling blast of her madness and hatred. 'It will now,' continued her ladyship, 'be given to me.'

Her words seemed to hang in the cold air. Ace was almost amused at her incredible affrontery. Even the Cyber Leader seemed taken aback. Lady Peinforte, however, stared at the Doctor, impatiently awaiting his response.

Ace stepped forward. 'Listen, you old bag,' she began.

'Enough,' said Richard sharply.

Ace ignored him. 'The Doctor's not going to just give the statue to you.'

There was a silence. Ace turned to the Doctor for his confirmation. Something in his face made her blood run cold. She wavered. 'Tell her, Doctor,' she said, with a note of fear.

The Doctor looked down at the ground and said nothing. He appeared to be weighing up the choices in his mind. This was no time for silence. Ace shook his arm. 'Doctor?' she said again loudly. This time she did not bother to conceal that she was imploring him.

'Doctor . . . who?' asked Lady Peinforte. She smiled malevolently at Ace. 'Haven't you ever wondered where he came from?' She swung round and faced the Doctor fully. 'And who he is?'

Ace began to tremble. 'Nobody knows who the Doctor is,' she said, as firmly as she could manage to do so.

'Except me,' said Lady Peinforte.

There are moments when time stands still. Indeed, the Doctor himself was not only an authority on why such a phenomenon should occur but was additonally capable of engineering such an event quite deliberately. This, however, was not a moment he had the slightest wish of contriving, as Ace could tell at once from the expression on his ashen face when he eventually looked up. It was one she had never seen there before, and it took her some seconds to realize that she was seeing for the first time a look of defeat in the Doctor's eyes.

Ace was mesmerized by the Doctor. 'How?' she managed to whisper.

'From the statue,' said Lady Peinforte triumphantly. 'It is his creation.'

'All right,' began Ace. 'So what does it matter? He's a Time Lord. I know that.'

Lady Peinforte smiled almost kindly on her. 'And you think that is all,' she said sweetly. She turned to the Doctor and her expression became one of cold fury. 'Well, Doctor?'

There was a moment before the Doctor could reply. 'If I give you the statue?' he said finally. His voice was almost inaudible.

Lady Peinforte's voice was like silk. 'Your power becomes mine.' Her eyes hardened. 'But your secrets remain your own.'

The Doctor slowly turned to Ace and put his hands on her shoulders. He looked sadly into her eyes. 'It's all over, Ace. My battle; all my battles: I've lost, I can only surrender.'

131

'Yes,' Lady Peinforte agreed calmly.

The Doctor turned and faced her. 'But not,' he said, 'to you. The Cybermen will have the Nemesis.'

The Cyber Leader was clearly surprised. 'This is most rational, Doctor,' he said.

Lady Peinforte appeared to be on the verge of a fit. 'But . . . but I know your secret,' she blurted.

The Doctor looked her full in the eyes. In all the moments that would ever come, Ace doubted whether she ever saw him looking more magnificent. 'Very well,' he replied in total defiance. 'Tell them.'

Lady Peinforte put her hand to her forehead. She could no longer comprehend the world. Her voice became pathetic. 'But I know . . .' she repeated softly, almost speaking to herself.

The Doctor was now fully in command of himself. 'I'm afraid,' he replied magisterially, and drawing himself up to his full height, 'that makes only two of us.'

The Cyber Leader stepped forward impatiently. 'You may now give me the bow, Doctor,' he grated.

'Very well,' the Doctor replied.

Ace could not believe her ears. 'You can't, Doctor,' she shouted desperately.

For once Lady Peinforte was in complete agreement with her. 'No,' she repeated, 'you cannot.'

The Doctor, however, ignored them, and in deathly silence handed the silver bow to the Cyber Leader.

'Deactivate its destructive capability,' ordered the Cyber Leader.

The Doctor turned obediently to the statue. 'Do you understand the Cyber leader's order?' he asked.

'Perfectly,' replied the statue in its cold, calm voice.

Ace looked on in growing horror. 'You can't do this, Doctor,' she said.

The Doctor gave no sign of having heard her. The Cyber leader placed the bow in the statue's hands. He stood back almost reverently. 'Prepare it for launching to liaise with our fleet,' he commanded the Doctor. 'You have its position from this device.'

He was indicating Ace's ghetto blaster. He pressed a button on the front and ejected the jazz cassette. The Cyber Leader removed it and held it tauntingly in front of Ace and the Doctor. 'A new and final era begins, Doctor,' he said. 'Imagination, thought, freedom, pleasure, all will end.' He crushed the tape in his fist and dropped the broken pieces to the ground. He addressed the group in general. 'The Earth will be transformed into our base planet, the new Mondas,' he anounced. 'Before I kill you all, you may watch the arrival of our fleet. Launch the Nemesis.'

Ace screamed, a final plea. 'Don't do it, Doctor! Please, please don't.' It was hopeless. Again, the Doctor gave not the slightest indication of having heard her. Instead he stepped forward to the sled and pressed the switches, activating the rockets. He stepped back again and stood clear. The rockets began to hum. Lady Peinforte stared in horrified disbelief.

'It's about to launch,' the Doctor warned them grimly. 'Keep back.'

The rockets were building up power, and their steady whine turned into a muted roar. The Doctor stood watching the statue expressionlessly. Suddenly, Lady Peinforte gave an unearthly piercing shriek and

133

running forward threw herself on to the statue. Richard moved towards her, shouting 'No, lady,' but it was too late. There was a blinding flash of radiant light as Lady Peinforte and the statue shimmered and then coalesced. The rockets fired and the statue of Nemesis was launched once again to return into space.

When it had faded into the sky, Ace and Richard found themselves looking at each other in shock, as was the Doctor. Only the Cyber Leader appeared calm. 'We shall watch its progress,' he said smoothly to the Doctor.

'Certainly,' the Doctor replied with perfect self-control. He switched on the ghetto blaster's holographic display, and a hologram began to take form once again immediately above the machine. They all began to watch.

Many hundreds of dots could be seen around the Moon. The Cybermen's fleet had been augmented since the last viewing, and its ships hung in space like a swarm. From the Earth another, single and smaller, dot appeared, approaching the very centre of the fleet. The nearer it grew, the brighter the Nemesis became, until it was glowing so brightly that the other dots were becoming less visible.

Then it exploded.

The entire hologram was instantly flooded with a dazzling, impossibly bright white light which slowly faded until only the occasional star glittered distantly in the awesome reaches of silent space. The Cyber Leader involuntarily stepped forward. He passed his hand through the image in utter disbelief, but the Doctor, who had taken off his spectacles and polished them on his handkerchief, was now gazing at him in quiet satisfaction.

'No . . .' grated the Cyber Leader.

'Yes,' replied the Doctor firmly. 'The fleet has been destroyed.'

'But . . . how?'

'Simple.'

'The Nemesis was under my command. I ordered it only to liaise with our force.'

'Ah, but I had ordered the Nemesis to destroy it. When you took control and changed the instruction through me, I simply asked the statue whether it understood what you said; I didn't say anything to it about obeying you.'

The Leader looked murderously at the diminutive figure in front of him. 'Then you will join them,' he said, aiming his laser at the Doctor's head.

The Doctor shrugged. 'Worth it,' he said simply, and closed his eyes.

As he did so, Richard seized his chance. He pulled out the gold-headed arrow that had been embedded in the door of the TARDIS since the first battle on the building site, and rushed forward. The Cyber Leader's finger was tightening on the trigger as Richard shoved the arrow with all his strength into the chest panel. The Leader dropped his weapon and fell writhing to the ground, rattling wildly.

The Doctor opened his eyes. 'Goodbye,' he said.

The Cyber Leader was still.

The Doctor slapped Richard on the back. 'That seems to be that,' he said. 'Thank you.'

Richard nodded. 'It's nothing, master. I wish only

that I could have saved my lady also. But she was one with your statue.' He looked away sadly across the muddy, grotesque terrain: the half-built modern houses, the cement mixers and excavators. 'How shall I live now?' he asked. 'Stranded here, a stranger in this time.'

The Doctor nodded sympathetically. 'I know just how you feel,' he agreed. 'However . . .'

But Ace beat him to it. 'We'll give you a lift,' she said brightly.

Richard clearly did not understand.

'Take you back,' translated the Doctor.

Richard looked at him in wonder. 'Is't possible?' he whispered.

'Anything's possible,' smiled the Doctor.

'Why,' said Richard, 'methinks I hear celestial music.'

The Doctor, no stranger to these imaginings, smiled indulgently. 'And I'd like to buy you a drink on the way,' he added. 'If you've got the time.'

Richard smiled broadly. 'No Doctor,' he said firmly. 'I shall buy you a drink.'

'In that case I know just the place,' said the Doctor. 'Speaking of celestial music . . .'

11

In the pub garden, their table was still free and the perfect summer's day uninterrupted as Ace and the Doctor took their seats. The ten-minute interval was just drawing to an end.

'Perfect timing,' smiled the Doctor.

Ace looked through the crowd to the bar where, despite her reservations, Richard seemed to be getting served without any difficulty. She had after all coached him in what to say to the person he insisted on referring to as the Potman, but the Doctor's lengthy lecture on the history and appreciation of jazz, which was taking place simultaneously, had been no small interference. The band reappeared and picked up their instruments. Before they recommenced, however, and before Richard could return, there were matters Ace wanted to clarify. 'So you sent the Nemesis into space to draw the Cybermen so you could finish them off?' she said.

The Doctor waved to the saxophone player. 'I suppose I did,' he answered with apparent surprise. 'How clever of me.'

'But then you forgot.'

'That's it, yes.'

Richard was approaching through the crowd with the drinks. There was hardly any time. Ace leaned close to the Doctor and spoke quietly. 'But there's still one question you haven't answered,' she said.

The Doctor did not appear to hear her. Instead, he turned and smiled over his shoulder to Richard, who was now very near. 'Here he is now,' he said.

Richard placed the glasses carefully on the table and sat down. 'My apparel excites great interest,' he said.

There was a roll from the drums. The saxophone player looked round at the quartet and they came to order, awaiting the count-in.

The Doctor leaned to Richard. 'I think you'll like this,' he said encouragingly. Richard smiled and sat back, giving the band his full attention.

'Professor!' whispered Ace in exasperation. 'Doctor!'

The Doctor put a finger to his lips. The saxophone player began to count. 'One, two . . .'

Ace was not, as usual, to be put off. She put her mouth to the Doctor's ear and, with great determination, asked: '*Who are you?*'

The Doctor momentarily turned to her and, for the briefest moment, she thought she was actually going to get an answer. Then he winked and smiled as, in perfect time, the band began to play.